BUSHW

As another bullet smashed through the window and whined viciously off the iron stove, Drake threw the table aside and ducked behind the window.

He looked at the Pinkerton.

The man had a bad cut across his forehead, but the scarlet splash of blood on his right shoulder spoke of a more severe wound.

Drake removed the five .44-40 shells from Withers's pocket and reloaded his Colt. He hammered two fast shots out the window, firing at rain and wind.

Withers stirred and groaned.

Drake knelt beside him.

It looked like the bushwhacker's bullet had entered the meat of the man's right shoulder, ranged upward, then exited at his collarbone before burning across his forehead.

"Wha-what's happening?" the Pinkerton asked.

A bullet slammed into the cabin, then another.

"Somebody's trying to kill you, Withers, or both of us."

Ralph Compton

The Burning Range

A Ralph Compton Novel
by Joseph A. West

A SIGNET BOOK

SIGNET

Published by New American Library, a division of
Penguin Group (USA) Inc., 375 Hudson Street,
New York, New York 10014, USA
Penguin Group (Canada), 90 Eglinton Avenue East, Suite 700, Toronto,
Ontario M4P 2Y3, Canada (a division of Pearson Penguin Canada Inc.)
Penguin Books Ltd., 80 Strand, London WC2R 0RL, England
Penguin Ireland, 25 St. Stephen's Green, Dublin 2,
Ireland (a division of Penguin Books Ltd.)
Penguin Group (Australia), 250 Camberwell Road, Camberwell, Victoria 3124,
Australia (a division of Pearson Australia Group Pty. Ltd.)
Penguin Books India Pvt. Ltd., 11 Community Centre, Panchsheel Park,
New Delhi - 110 017, India
Penguin Group (NZ), 67 Apollo Drive, Rosedale, North Shore 0632,
New Zealand (a division of Pearson New Zealand Ltd.)
Penguin Books (South Africa) (Pty.) Ltd., 24 Sturdee Avenue,
Rosebank, Johannesburg 2196, South Africa

Penguin Books Ltd., Registered Offices:
80 Strand, London WC2R 0RL, England

First published by Signet, an imprint of New American Library,
a division of Penguin Group (USA) Inc.

First Printing, December 2010
10   9   8   7   6   5   4   3   2   1

THE IMMORTAL COWBOY

This is respectfully dedicated to the "American Cowboy." His was the saga sparked by the turmoil that followed the Civil War, and the passing of more than a century has by no means diminished the flame.

True, the old days and the old ways are but treasured memories, and the old trails have grown dim with the ravages of time, but the spirit of the cowboy lives on.

In my travels—to Texas, Oklahoma, Kansas, Nebraska, Colorado, Wyoming, New Mexico, and Arizona—I always find something that reminds me of the Old West. While I am walking these plains and mountains for the first time, there is this feeling that a part of me is eternal, that I have known these old trails before. I believe it is the undying spirit of the frontier calling me, through the mind's eye, to step back into time. What is the appeal of the Old West of the American frontier?

It has been epitomized by some as the dark and bloody period in American history. Its heroes—Crockett, Bowie, Hickok, Earp—have been reviled and criticized. Yet the Old West lives on, larger than life.

It has become a symbol of freedom, when there was always another mountain to climb and another river to cross; when a dispute between two men was settled not with expensive lawyers, but with fists, knives, or guns. Barbaric? Maybe. But some things never change. When the cowboy rode into the pages of American history, he left behind a legacy that lives within the hearts of us all.

—*Ralph Compton*

Chapter 1

When a gambler is trying to outrun a losing streak he sometimes forgets the rules. That night Chauncey Drake misplaced two of them: He was playing poker under a blood moon, always unlucky for him, and he'd stubbed his toe on a dead man.

In more prosperous times, he'd have sat out the unlucky night in his hotel room with a bottle and a couple of whores who were a credit to their profession.

But these were not thriving days for Chauncey Drake.

And he suspected that harder times were coming down.

"The game," Peter J. Grapples said, "is poker."

The eyes peering over the top of the banker's glasses nudged Drake gently. A man doesn't push a known and named gunfighter too much.

"I'm studying on it," Drake said, staring at his cards.

"It's not difficult, Mr. Drake," Grapples said. "I raised you ten."

"Man's got the right to take his time," Ed Winslow said.

"But not all night," Grapples said.

Winslow nodded. "No, not all night. Truer words were never spoken."

Drake studied his cards. Aces and eights, a dead man's hand.

Nothing about the damned night boded well.

Grapples wasn't pushing him hard, and Drake understood why.

But what the banker didn't know was that Drake's blue Colt currently reposed in Sy Goldberg's Pawn and Mercantile on Second Street, tagged, bagged, and pigeonholed.

In return for the revolver, Drake had received, from Sy's own hand, as befitted a regular customer, a ticket and ten dollars.

The ten dollars now sat in front of him, and there was not another thin dime in his poke.

Ed Winslow's eyes moved to the saloon window. "Blackest night I've seen in a spell," he said. He cocked his head, listening into the darkness. "Coyotes are hunting close."

"There's blood on the moon," Grapples said.

"Unlucky for some," Winslow said.

"Maybe for you, Mr. Drake," Grapples said, smiling. "Or me."

The banker's smile faded and he sighed. "The game is poker," he said for a second time.

Drake made up his mind.

He pushed his ten into the pot. "I call." He spread his cards. "Got me a dead man."

"Too little and way too late," Grapples said. He tossed his hand onto the table. "Three ladies."

"Unlucky for some," Winslow said.

Grapples gathered up the deck. "Shall I deal?"

Drake shook his head. "I'm done."

He rose to his feet, a slim man of medium height, dressed in patched and faded gambler's finery.

"Another time, perhaps," Grapples said.

Drake nodded. "Yes, another time."

He walked to the door and stepped outside.

The blood moon was rising, but for the moment it had spiked itself on a pine at the edge of town. The night gathered close and along First Street, kerosene lamps glowed red in the darkness and smoked like the cinders of fallen stars.

Drake found a ragged cigar stub in the pocket of his frockcoat, then took a seat in one of the rockers scattered along the saloon porch.

Across the street, outside the marshal's office, the dead man was propped up in a pine coffin, illuminated by the railroad lantern on the boardwalk in front of him.

The man's face was as blue as marble, his eye sockets pooled in shadow, and he showed his teeth in a death grimace.

The reason for the grotesque display was that when Marshal Dub Halloran killed a man in the line of duty, justice had to be seen, by the whole town, to be done.

The dead man was a small-time thief and all-around nuisance by the name of Bates or Baxter—nobody knew for sure.

He'd stolen a side of bacon from a farmer's smokehouse, and Halloran had tracked the man to a box canyon north of the farm. Bates or Baxter had promptly surrendered, but, for convenience' sake, the marshal had gunned him where he stood and dragged the body back to town behind his horse.

Nobody much cared. Sy Goldberg pretty much summed up the town's attitude when he declared that the man's death was a case of "good riddance to bad rubbish."

Drake didn't have much sympathy for Bates or Baxter either.

On his way to the saloon he'd tripped over the man's coffin, and everybody knew how unlucky that was.

Drake took a last draw on his cigar and ground it out under his shoe.

He was busted. Broke. Destitute. Penniless. And it hurt.

He'd sold his horse a while back, then his watch, then his diamond stickpin, then his emerald ring. Sy Goldberg had his Colt and the shoulder holster that went with it.

Farther down the street he saw the lights of the Bon-Ton Hotel. He couldn't go back there until the manager left for the night. The man had been pressing Drake for money and had threatened to padlock his room if the eighty dollars he owed was not paid "instanter or even sooner."

A six-month losing streak had exacted its toll, and that night Drake knew he had scraped the bottom of his last barrel.

He rose to his feet and stepped to the edge of the boardwalk.

A cowboy walked past, leading his horse, neither looking to his left nor right. He was followed by one of the respectable matrons of the town. Drake touched his hat to the woman, but she lifted her nose and ignored him.

Despite his gloom, Drake smiled. Could people sense

poverty? Or did they not care to look at a man who was wrapped up in his own gloomy shadow?

Round as a coin, the moon had broken free of the pines and was riding high in the sky, spawning crouching shadows all over town. Out in the darkness coyotes yipped, their fur rippled by a rising wind.

Drake was seized by the urge to flee, to steal a horse and outrun the tiger. But flee to where? To yet another hick town in the middle of nowhere, where no one would be glad at his coming or sad at his leaving?

From the frying pan into the fire.

"Evening, Chauncey. Still prospering, I see, huh?"

Drake turned. Savannah Swan stood on the boardwalk, a smile on her scarlet lips.

"That obvious?"

"I'd say. You've mended them britches you're wearing so many times they look like Grandma's patchwork quilt."

Drake said nothing, and Savannah said, "Still trying to buck a losing deck?"

"That sums it up."

"Let me buy you a drink."

"I'll pass."

That sounded harsh and Drake sweetened it with a smile. "How's business?"

The woman shrugged. "Tuesday night. It's slow. All the married ones are home with their skinny wives and the drovers don't get paid till Friday."

"Things are tough all over," Drake said.

Savannah ignored that and said, "Why don't you talk to Loretta?"

Drake shook his head. "Loretta ain't exactly a whore with a heart of gold. She stung me on my ring."

"She likes you, Chauncey. And I know she's holding. Got a big roll."

"Smooth that out for me."

"Like I said, she's holding. Ask her for a grubstake."

"I've got no, what they call, collateral. Loretta has my ring and Sy Goldberg has my gun."

"So? You ain't going anyplace, are you?"

"Loretta is holding, you say?"

"Big roll."

"I'll study on it."

Savannah smiled. "Don't study on it too long. She's leaving town tomorrow to visit a sick aunt—be gone for a week."

"She's home right now?"

"Washing her hair. She's had no gentlemen callers and isn't expecting any."

"Maybe I'll go talk to her."

Savannah smiled, looking over Drake's shabby clothes and down-at-heel shoes. "Maybe you should."

She gathered her shawl around her naked shoulders. "I've got to get down to the Alamo. There will be no customers, but Hank Bowman expects me to be there on the chance that somebody gets horny."

The woman glanced at the sky and shivered as she walked away. "Blood on the moon, Chauncey," she said over her shoulder.

"Yeah, I noticed that," Drake said.

Chapter 2

Loretta Sinclair lived in a gingerbread house on the edge of town. The place had two stories, a covered porch, and a small garden that grew a fine crop of bunchgrass and cactus.

As whores go, Loretta was more successful than most and she charged top dollar. Her great height, six foot four in her spike-heeled boots, added to her attraction and had earned her the nickname High Timber.

"Hell, when she stood next to me, the top of my head only reached her bush." Drake had heard one over-awed customer say.

Loretta and her high timber had many admirers, and her sprawling house with a carriage and matched pair out back in the barn testified to her popularity and prosperity.

Drake stopped, straightened his celluloid collar, and smoothed his mustache. He removed his plug hat, licked his fingers, and patted down his hair. He was wishful for lavender water but had none.

He settled the hat back on his head and looked at

the moon. It was still red against the sky, like a drop of blood on black velvet.

The wind gusted, flapping the legs of his pants, and it smelled of shadowed places and dead things.

It seemed that every oil lamp in Loretta's house was lit and elongated rectangles of yellow light spilled onto the sand of the yard.

Suddenly Drake became aware of the hopelessness of his mission and deep inside, little bits of him began to curl up and die.

Loretta Sinclair was a whore with a heart of iron, a cold-eyed businesswoman with no good reason to grub-stake a bum.

Drake swallowed hard, put one foot in front of the other, and slowly walked toward the door.

He would have to rely on his charm. And, as soon as that thought crossed his mind, he knew with an awful certainty that his empty words would fall on the deaf ears of a woman who had heard it all before.

Drake knuckled the oak-and-glass door and waited.

The groaning wind tugged at him, trying to drag him away from there.

He knocked again.

Nothing.

Amazed at his own boldness, or desperation, Drake turned the polished brass doorknob and stuck his head inside.

"Miz Loretta, are you home?" he called out.

He was answered by an echoing silence, as though the house was holding its breath. Waiting.

"It's me! Chauncey Drake, as ever was!"

In the quiet his voice boomed, hollow as a drum.

Drake waited a few moments, then tried again, louder this time into the hush. "Miss Loretta!"

No answer.

Savannah Swan had said Loretta was home. Then where the hell was she?

Drake stepped inside and removed his hat.

There was a gilded, oval mirror on the wall to his left. He parted his hair in the middle with his fingers and smoothed it into place on each side of his head.

That accomplished, he didn't much like what he saw: a tired brown-eyed young man with an untrimmed mustache and the aggrieved look of a scolded puppy.

"Miss Loretta!"

Drake walked farther into the house. A parlor opened up to his left, and across the hall was a dining room. A carpeted stairway to the second floor rose in front of him.

"Miss Loretta! It's me, Chauncey Drake!"

The answering silence mocked him. Somewhere a clock ticked and at the back of the house a screen door slammed open and shut in the wind.

Maybe Loretta was outside, feeding the horses.

Drake walked past the stairway and along a narrow passage leading to the rear of the house. A door to his right was ajar and he glimpsed what appeared to be a bedroom dresser.

"Miss Loretta, are you in there?"

He looked inside. And froze in shock right where he stood.

Loretta Sinclair, naked, legs spread wide, was sprawled across the bed, her long damp hair forming an auburn halo around her head.

It was the seductive pose she might have adopted to welcome a client, or an ardent lover.

But the woman's whoring days were over. Her days for doing anything were over. The knife handle protruding from between her scarlet-splashed breasts gave proof of that.

On the wall, above the bed's headboard, two words were scrawled in blood.

GET OUT!

Drake, dazed, stepped to the bed, but stumbled over an overturned stool. He landed on top of Loretta's slippery body, then, horrified, lurched back to his feet.

A moment later a woman screamed.

Chapter 3

The scream was a primal shriek of fear, loud and grating.

Savannah Swan stood in the doorway. Her terrified eyes took in Drake's blood-soaked clothes and bloody hands; then she turned and ran, waving her hands over her head.

"Murder! Murder!"

"Wait!" Drake yelled. "Savannah, come back!"

He pounded after the woman, tripped on a rug and fell, then scrambled to his feet again.

By the time he got outside, Savannah was already running down the middle of First Street, holding her skirt above her knees.

"Murder! Murder!"

Panicked, his eyes wild, Drake was driven by an instinct to escape.

He ran back into the house, then dashed to the barn.

Loretta kept her horses there.

The two Morgans were dozing in their stalls and paid Drake no mind when he ran inside. Only silver moonlight blading through the barn door lit up the interior.

Frantic now, Drake searched around. He found a bridle and other tack on a wall, but no sign of a saddle.

But the bridle was all he needed.

He had the bit in the mouth of one of the Morgans when a man's voice stopped him.

"Stay right where you're at, Chauncey. Or I'll drop you, by God."

Drake turned and saw the long, lanky silhouette of Marshal Dub Halloran framed in the doorway. Moonlight gleamed on the blue barrel of his Remington.

"I didn't kill her, Dub," Drake said.

As though he hadn't heard, Halloran took a single step toward him. "Come out here, Chauncey. And keep your hand well away from your gun."

"I don't have a gun, Dub."

"Git out here, damn you, and don't back talk me!"

The bridle still in his left hand, Drake stepped forward and stopped when the moonlight fell on him.

Another man stomped into the barn, a shotgun in his hands.

"It's Loretta all right, Marshal," he said. "Stabbed through the heart with a bowie." Drake felt the man's eyes on him. "Was it him?"

"Yeah, he was trying to make a run for it." Halloran turned his head very slightly toward the other man. "Keep the Greener on him, Bill. He's mighty sudden."

"I got faith in this here scattergun, mister," the man called Bill said to Drake. "Make a fancy move an' I'll cut you off at the knees."

"Damn it, I didn't kill her," Drake said.

The barn was closing in on him and he felt trapped, struggling hard to breathe.

"Damn it, she was already dead when I found her."

Drake knew he was talking into the wind. Nobody was listening to him.

"Drop that bridle, then ease out your gun with two fingers of your left hand, Chauncey," Halloran said. "Do it real slow, now. I ain't taking any chances with you."

The marshal jammed the muzzle of the Remington into Drake's belly. "No first chances, no second chances."

"My gun's in Sy Goldberg's pawn," Drake said. "Search me if you want."

Halloran said, "Bill, see if he's heeled." The lawman's long, hangdog face looked like melting candle wax. He took a step back. "Chauncey, I see anything quick, I'll gun you."

"He's light, Dub," Bill said after his search. "He ain't carrying."

Halloran nodded toward the barn door. "Now, we're walking to the jail, real peaceful, like we was visiting kinfolk." He showed teeth under his mustache. "You know me, Chauncey. I ain't superstitious. Try to cut and run, and I'll shoot you right between the shoulder blades."

"Dub, you're one miserable son of a bitch," Drake said.

"Ain't I, though," the marshal said. "Live longer that way."

Chapter 4

Chauncey Drake woke in the gloom of his cell, aware of a small, warm weight on his chest.

He opened his eyes to the unblinking amber gaze of a tiny calico cat.

"How did you get in here?" Drake said.

The cat stared at him.

Drake said, "Through the window, huh? If a hole in the wall with iron bars in it can be called a window."

He stroked the calico's soft fur and was rewarded with a purr.

"Well, cat, you find me very low," Drake said. "They're going to hang me, you know." He shook his head. "Now that you have the facts, what's your considered opinion on that?"

The cat had none.

"I understand how you feel," Drake said. "I must say that the Honorable Peace Commission of the City of Green Meadow, Oklahoma, and Indian Territories, did give me a fair trial."

The calico blinked, stretched, then curled up on Drake's chest again, still staring at him.

"I was accused of raping and murdering a—please forgive me for using the word—whore. Don't that beat anything you ever saw or heard tell of?"

Drake rubbed the cat's small, pointed ears. "I didn't do it, of course. Somebody else did. Being a jail cat an' all, I know you've probably heard that before, but it's the gospel."

The calico yawned, showing pointed fangs in a pink mouth.

"The real killer wrote 'Get out' on the wall in blood," Drake said. "Now why would he do that? Of course, my lawyer used it to try and get my neck out of the noose, said only a crazy person would write that on the wall. 'Gentlemen,' he said, 'my client is a nut, and you can't hang a nut.' But the honorable commissioners didn't see it that way. 'The sight of the gallows will soon restore the accused to his senses,' said Sy Goldberg, who has my gun in his pawn. 'The rope is the sovereign remedy for all cases of insanity, derangement, craziness, and loss of reason.' Well, that was yesterday, and now they're going to hang me in two days."

Drake looked into the cat's glowing eyes. "Don't seem hardly fair, do it? I mean, hanging a man for nothing."

"Who the hell are you talking to, Chauncey?"

Drake turned his head and saw Dub Halloran standing at the cell door.

"Cat," he said.

The marshal's eyes were growing accustomed to the gloom. "Oh, yeah, I see it. That damn cat hangs around.

I feed it sometimes when I feel like it, but usually I just kick it out of my damned way."

"You're a wonderful human being, Dub," Drake said.

"Get up. Bring your cup over here."

Drake swung his legs off his cot and the calico took this as her cue to leave and scrabbled through the cell window.

He threw the coffee dregs onto the dirt floor and stepped to the bars. "I could use some coffee."

"Hell, this is better than coffee."

Halloran held up a bottle. "Old Crow. The genuine article. Better than that rotgut you've been drinking in recent times." The marshal's grin was as warm as a rattler's. "And there's more where this came from. Now give me your damned cup."

Halloran took the tin cup, poured four fingers, and passed it back through the bars.

"What do you want, Dub?" Drake said, drinking.

"Want? I don't want nothing."

"Then who sent the whiskey? The honorable commissioners?"

"You nailed that, Chauncey. Fastened that right down, boy. Nobody ever said you wasn't smart. Loco, yeah, but not stupid."

"What do the commissioners want?"

"The town fathers, Chauncey. Sounds better."

"What do they want?"

"They want you to die real good," Halloran said, "like a decent Christian."

Chapter 5

Marshal Halloran read the question on Drake's face.

"Give the folks a show, Chauncey. That's all we ask."

"What kind of show?" Drake shoved his cup through the bars. "Fill that."

After he'd poured the whiskey, Halloran said, "For starters, don't die yellow."

"That ain't likely."

"Meaning, you will or you won't?"

"I won't give you the satisfaction of dying yellow, Dub."

"Good, then we're halfway there."

"What else do they want?"

"A good speech, Chauncey. When you stand on the gallows, tell the crowd that whiskey and whores has brought you to this pass."

"That's not far from the truth."

"Then say something like, 'But I had a good mother.' The women love that. Talk about your white-haired ma back on the farm, Chauncey, and about how it will break her poor old heart when she hears you got hanged."

Drake said, "My ma ran away with a corsets drummer when I was six."

"Damn it, Chauncey. The crowd doesn't have to know that. Listen, the town has bought red, white, and blue bunting for the gallows, paid for a new suit of clothes for the preacher, and ordered four barrels of beer and two meat hogs. There's big money involved here."

Drake said nothing, and Halloran said, "Will you do it?"

"Bring me another bottle and the makings."

"And?"

"And I'll die game."

"The speech?"

"I'll make my poor old ma back on the farm proud of me."

"Crackerjack, Chauncey! You're true blue, boy, like I always knew you was. It's going to be a pleasure and an honor to hang you."

After Halloran left, Drake said aloud, "The hell with you and the town fathers, Dub. I aim to squeal like a pig all the way to the drop."

There was no time in a jail cell, just the passage of dark to light and back again. Some condemned men tried to hold back the darkness and struggle mightily to spend just one more day in the light.

Chauncey Drake was not one of those.

In a death cell, a sense of helplessness that crushes the soul is the wheel that moves within a wheel, grinding slowly, destroying joy, annihilating hope.

All Drake wished to do now was die and get the damned thing over.

He was thirty-five years old that summer, a man with

no past and less future. The world would not mourn a failed, somewhat seedy gambler, or feel a sense of loss at his passing.

Drake sat on the edge of his cot and built a cigarette. Two bottles of Old Crow, one full, one empty, stood sentinel at his feet.

Moonlight, thin as mother's milk, spilled through the cell window and splashed on the floor. Far off the coyotes were calling and the wind prowled around the marshal's office and rattled the wood shingles on the roof.

Drake thumbed a match into flame and lit his cigarette, crimson light flaring briefly on the lean planes of his unshaven face.

He wished the calico cat would visit again. She'd not been much on conversation, but he'd enjoyed the closeness of another living creature, even a silent one.

Reaching down, Drake picked up the bottle and took a swig.

When was he due to hang?

Today? Tomorrow? The next day?

He couldn't remember.

He shook his head. Dying wasn't so bad. Doing it in public was.

The crowd would stuff their faces with pork and beer and then watch him dance at the end of a rope.

No matter how you cut it, it was a hell of a way for a man to cash out.

A key clanked in the cell-door lock.

Now? Was it now? But it was still dark.

"On your feet, Chauncey."

Dub Halloran's voice.

Drake rose, the cot creaking. "Is it time?"

He was irritated to hear the quaver in his voice.

Chapter 6

Halloran stepped into the cell. "Hell, no. You're out of here."

The marshal saw Drake's confusion.

"You know Jim Waters. Farm's out by Rock Creek?"

Still dazed, Drake shook his head.

"Well, he had a real pretty wife, until early this morning that is, when somebody raped and murdered her."

"Where . . . where was Waters?"

"In town. Getting supplies and three yards of gingham cloth for his wife."

Drake tried to collect thoughts scrambled by shock and bourbon.

"What happened?"

"Stella Waters—that was her name—was found by her husband naked and dead in their bedroom. She had a knife in her chest, her tits were cut off, and somebody had carved words on her forehead."

Halloran studied Drake for a few moments, then said, "Want to know what they were—the words, I mean?" Without waiting for an answer, he said, "'Get Out.'"

It was a lot of information for a confused brain to process and Drake said nothing.

The marshal filled in the silence.

"The city fathers say there is now grave doubt that you're guilty of murdering Loretta Sinclair. But you ain't real popular, Chauncey."

"How come?"

"The town is stuck with four barrels of beer, two meat hogs, an overdressed preacher, and nobody to hang."

"My heart breaks for the town."

"Sy Goldberg said we should string you up anyhow, since you got to be guilty of something, but the rest wouldn't go along with that. Still, you're surely a disappointment to everybody, Chauncey."

"Someday remind me to put a bullet into good ol' Sy," Drake said.

"Have to ask him to give you your gun back first."

He reached out and took the Old Crow from Drake's hand. "Your freeloading days are over, boy. Now get dressed and come into the office. I've got something for you."

Halloran had roughly handled Drake during his arrest, and his celluloid collar was ruined. He dropped it on the floor, shrugged into his frockcoat, and picked up his plug hat from the bed.

Halloran sat behind his desk, a carpetbag in front of him. "Chauncey, you ain't off the hook yet," he said. "There are them who reckon you might have an accomplice, the one who murdered Stella Waters."

"What do you think, Dub?"

"I don't think anything. When the city fathers order me to think, then I'll think."

"I didn't kill Loretta Sinclair, and I sure as hell don't have an accomplice who murdered a farmer's wife."

Halloran shrugged. "Maybe, maybe not. But if'n I was you, which I ain't, thank God, I'd light a shuck out of town fast as I could."

Drake allowed himself a small smile. "And go where?"

"Where your kind is always headed, Chauncey—hell."

Before Drake could say anything, the marshal nodded to the carpetbag. "Otto Grunwald brought that over from the Bon-Ton. He said there's nothing in it except a pair of drawers, a dirty shirt, and a razor. Said it wasn't worth keeping."

"I owe him money," Drake said.

"Figured that."

Halloran watched Drake pick up the bag. "A pair of drawers and a dirty shirt ain't much for a man to show for his life."

"Dub," Drake said, "that's the first sensible thing I've ever heard you say."

Chapter 7

On his way out, Drake glanced at the clock above Halloran's desk. It said eight fifteen.

He'd nothing to do and all night to do it in.

Drake found a rocker outside the saloon where he'd bumped into Savannah Swan the night Loretta Sinclair died and sat down.

Halloran had taken away his whiskey but not the makings. He set the carpetbag at his feet and built a cigarette.

To the north, the Sans Bois Mountains were lost in darkness and distance, but a dim throb of thunder echoed around their peaks and lightning flashed in the sky.

Thrown by an oil lamp, Drake's shadow capered on the boardwalk, more alive than the man who cast it.

But he smoked and laid his plans.

Tonight: Sleep in the livery stable.

Tomorrow: Head out of town.

The next day: He had no idea.

As a plan goes, it was not much, but it was all he had.

Drake turned as heels sounded on the boardwalk to
his left. He looked and felt his eyes get wide.

"Are you Mr. Drake?" the woman said.

Choking on his own desire, Drake could say nothing.

"I'm looking for Mr. Chauncey Drake," the woman
said, slightly irritated.

She had red hair, green eyes, the bright beauty of a
candle flame.

"That's me," Drake managed finally.

"I need—what do you people call it?—a pistol fighter.
I was told you fit the bill, and therefore I wish to hire
you."

Drake rose to his feet, smiled, and wished he'd
trimmed his mustache.

"I'm so very available," he said, his tone implying
more than the spoken word.

The woman recognized the implication and brushed
it aside.

"Mr. Drake, don't talk pretties to me. Don't try to be
smart, witty, or charming, since you'll fail on all those
counts. I wish to hire a ruffian with a gun, that is all. If
you feel you are qualified for the post, tell me now. If
you feel you are not, then step aside and let me pass."

Stung, Drake said, "Who do you want me to kill?"

"Hopefully, no one. Do you want the job?"

"What does it pay?"

A moment's hesitation, then the woman said, "One
thousand dollars. Five hundred in advance, the remainder when you are dismissed."

The amount hit Drake like a sledgehammer.

"I want the job," he said.

The woman's eyes, cool as mint, appraised him from his toes to the crown of his hat. "I thought you might," she said.

She gathered up her gray afternoon dress, preparing to cross the dusty street. "My name is Helen E. Lee," she said. "I bear a hero's name."

Drake smiled. "I bear a duck's name."

"Don't try to be funny, Mr. Drake," the woman said. "I'm not paying you to be funny. Now follow me, and stay alert."

As he picked up his carpetbag, Drake asked himself, Alert for what?

He didn't know it then, but the answer to that question was already stalking the dark distances.

Drake hesitated before entering the hotel lobby.

"Miss Lee, I'm not what you'd call real welcome here," he said.

"I paid your bill, Mr. Drake, and reserved you a room next to mine." She looked at him. "It was Mr. Grunwald who told me of your reputation with a gun. I don't know if you should thank him or not. Only time will answer that question."

"Are you trying to scare me?" Drake asked.

"Do you scare easily?"

"As easily as the next man."

"Then, for as long as you're in my employ, you'll be scared."

"Well"—Drake smiled—"that's good to know."

"Mr. Drake, I'm paying you to be scared. If you don't want the job, I'll find someone else."

"I'll stick," Drake said.

Helen Lee's eyes were cold on his.

"If you take my money and run, you're a dead man. Do we understand each other?"

Drake gave a little bow. "Perfectly."

The woman turned and stepped into the hotel. Drake followed . . . like a puppy dog on a leash, he told himself.

"Drink?"

Drake nodded and Helen Lee poured three fingers of bourbon into a glass and handed it to him.

Her breasts were large, her waist tiny, corseted, Drake decided, and her full lips were glistening, like a woman who waits to be kissed.

But Helen Lee's mind was not on romance, as the question she asked next revealed.

"How many men have you killed, Mr. Drake?" she asked.

"Adding them all up, the answer is none."

"Explain that."

"Miss Lee, when a man in my profession gets a reputation as a dangerous gunfighter, he encourages it. That way, other men are less apt to challenge him. You understand?"

Drake was glad to see that Helen Lee suddenly looked a little off balance. So she was human after all.

"But Mr. Grunwald says you killed a famous gunman named Whitey Forbes."

Drake tried his whiskey. It was smooth and good.

"Whitey Forbes was a blowhard, all wind and piss. I shot at him and he fell down. Not from my bullet, but from fright. Last I heard, Whitey is tending bar in Denver."

His eyes lifted to the woman's face.

"Miss Lee, I've been in two gunfights. One with Whitey Forbes, the other with a man named Shannon down El Paso way. We were both drunk, but I managed to shoot him in the ankle." He sipped from his glass. "I was aiming at his thick skull."

Drake looked at her. "Still want me to take the job?"

"God help me, but you're all I've got," Helen Lee said.

Chapter 8

"A touching vote of confidence," Drake said.

"I don't have much confidence in you, Mr. Drake. I suspect you may lack the one quality I need."

"What's that?"

"Courage."

"A man doesn't know how brave he'll be until he's put to the test."

"And I plan to test you. Mr. Drake, your job is to keep me alive. The two women who died, the whore and the farmer's wife, that was only the beginning. There are destructive forces at work here, unleashed by rich and powerful men."

Drake rose from his chair and helped himself to whiskey.

"Why would anyone want to kill you, Miss Lee?" he asked.

"Because I know what is at stake."

"What's at stake?"

"I can't tell you, not now. I can tell you that a vast amount of money—millions—is involved."

Drake smiled. "This hick town is worth millions?"

"Yes. That, and perhaps much, much more."

"Why?"

"As I said, I can't tell you."

Helen Lee moved past Drake and the warm, female smell of her filled his head. She was, he decided, the most desirable woman he'd ever known.

"Come over here, Mr. Drake," she said.

Drake rose and walked to the dresser, where the woman had placed an envelope, his Colt, shoulder rig, and a box of .44-40 shells on its scarred top.

He looked at the gun. "You sure seem to know a lot about my affairs."

"Only what I need to know."

"And Sy gave you my gun without a pawn ticket, huh?"

"Yes, he was most cooperative. He says you're one of his best customers."

"That didn't stop him from wanting to hang me."

Helen Lee smiled. "He mentioned it. He said to tell you that Sy the city father wanted you hanged, not Sy the pawnbroker and your friend."

"When I put a bullet into his fat belly, I'll be sure to tell him I'm only shooting Sy the city father."

Drake loaded the Colt from the box, stuck it in his waistband, and picked up the shoulder holster. Helen Lee handed him the envelope.

"Five hundred on account," she said.

Drake took the money. "Where do we go from here?"

"Your room adjoins mine. You will not, under any circumstances, leave it while I am in residence. And you will forsake the gambling tables."

"And when you go out?"

"You will come with me."

"Well, that could be interesting."

Helen Lee's face was stiff. "Don't get any ideas, Mr. Drake. I find you a singularly unattractive man."

Drake shook his head, smiling inwardly. Now he was a spanked puppy dog.

"There is one more thing," the woman said.

"I'm listening."

"There is a vile creature involved in all this who goes by the name of the Fat Man. In the unlikely event that everything turns bad, don't let me fall into his hands. Kill me first. Do you understand?"

"Who is he?"

"I can't tell you, not yet. Will you do as I say?"

Drake nodded. "Well, if everything goes to hell, I'll kill you—or gun the Fat Man."

"You won't. The Fat Man can't be killed. He's much too powerful."

Drake opened his mouth to speak, but Helen Lee cut him short. "Here is the key to your room. You are dismissed for the time being."

"Thankee, Miss Lee," Drake said, knuckling his forehead.

The irony was lost on the woman. "I'll come for you in the morning. Be there."

Chapter 9

Chauncey Drake woke to darkness and unease.

He lay still for a few moments, listening.

The wind rattled the window in its casement and a flurry of rain drummed on the panes.

Naked, Drake got to his feet, picked up his Colt, and settled his hat on his head, a drover's habit he had picked up as a boy and had never lost.

On cat feet, he stepped to the window, pushed back the curtain, and looked outside.

Lamps guttered along First Street and gleamed on the wet boardwalk. Outside the shuttered New York Hat Shoppe, a barrel held a cluster of night-blooming flowers and next door the sign above Jim Reilly's Gun Store swayed and creaked on iron chains.

The only living thing on the street was a buckskin horse tied to the hotel hitching rail.

Then Drake heard the murmur of a man's voice. Coming from Helen Lee's room.

Light from the glass panel above his door glinted

blue on the gun in his hand as he stepped to the wall and listened.

He heard only fragments of conversation.

". . . our card rights, Helen . . . we'll win . . ."

". . . Waters's farm . . . need . . . important . . ."

". . . in the bag . . . he'll run . . ."

". . . Don't fail me . . ."

A pause, then the man spoke louder.

". . . meet with Rockefeller and Benz . . . tell them . . ."

". . . the Fat Man, Henry . . ."

". . . I'll deal with him . . . Helen . . . don't worry . . ."

The woman laughed, a derisive cackle that cut to the bone.

It was followed by the crack of a man's hard hand hitting a woman's face.

A voice rose. "Don't belittle me, you bitch!"

Drake judged where the man was standing and raised his gun.

But Helen Lee's sobbing voice stopped him.

"I'm sorry, Henry . . ."

The man called Henry's voice was still loud.

"I told you I'd take care of the Fat Man . . . will . . ."

"I know . . . sorry . . . Henry . . . always . . ."

Drake eased down the hammer of his Colt.

Henry's voice again. "The gambler . . ."

". . . expendable . . . idiot . . ."

The door of Helen Lee's room opened, closed.

Then silence.

Drake stood for a while, his head bent in thought. He crossed to his bed and lay down.

He didn't think he'd sleep much that night. But he did.

And that was a bad mistake.

* * *

It was full daylight when Drake woke.

He dressed quickly, slid his Colt into the shoulder holster, and tapped on Helen Lee's door.

No answer.

Drake waited, tried again.

There was no sound within and Drake pushed open the door a few inches.

"Miss Lee?"

The woman didn't reply and Drake stepped inside. The early sun, thick with rain, lay dull on the windows but revealed an orderly room. There was no sign of forced entry, though clothing scattered across the floor gave evidence of a hurried departure.

Drake was puzzled. It seemed that Helen Lee had left without telling him. Why?

Drake closed the door and walked downstairs to the lobby.

Otto Grunwald stood behind the desk. The man looked sour and decided to be surly.

"What the hell do you want, Drake?"

"I'm looking for Miss Lee."

"She left two hours ago, said she was going riding."

"Did she say where?"

"What's it to you, Drake? I don't reveal the where-abouts of my guests."

Grunwald's eyes were unfriendly and belligerent behind his steel-rimmed glasses.

Drake was not entirely in a sociable mood himself and all the whiskey he'd drunk was finally beating up on him. He had the reputation of being a gunfighter, and maybe it was time to act like one.

"I don't understand you, Otto," he said.

"Who the hell cares? Don't understand what?"

The Colt left the holster like a striking snake and suddenly Grunwald found himself inhaling the muzzle, his eyes bugging as he heard the triple click of the hammer.

"I don't understand how a man who's about to get his goddamned head blowed off can be so uppity." Drake smiled. "Now, I'll ask you again, polite like—did Miss Lee say where she was headed?"

It took Grunwald a few moments to get his lips to move, then, "Honest, she didn't tell me. She said she was going out for a ride and to let you know that she'd be back before noon."

The man watched Drake holster his gun. "Miss Lee keeps her mare at the livery," he offered.

"Well, thank you, Otto," Drake said. "You're true blue. But if I find that you've been holding back on me, I'll come looking for you." He smiled again. "Understand?"

"Oh, yes, sir," Grunwald said.

He was a frightened man.

And for some reason he couldn't define, that troubled Drake greatly.

Chapter 10

"She headed west. That's all I can tell you."

"What's west?"

"Nothin'. Sodbusters, maybe."

And the farm where Stella Waters had been murdered.

The liveryman's name was Lister, a stove-up drover with a withered arm and the disposition of a caged cougar.

Behind Drake rain lashed across the open stable door and ticked from holes in the roof.

He made up his mind.

"I need to rent a horse," he said, "and an oilskin, if you have one."

"Got a hoss," Lister said. "Got no confidence you'll bring him back, though."

"Lay that out for me, mister," Drake said, his voice edged.

Lister scratched his hairy jaw and spat.

"Could be a man is suspicioned of murder. Could be that man might want to leave town and never come back." Lister nodded. "Yup, could be."

"I'll be back," Drake said.

"So you say."

"Let me see the damned horse."

"Suit yerself. Only he ain't for hire, not to you."

Lister led a rangy sorrel from a stall.

"I'll sell him, but I won't rent him."

"How much?"

"Finest piece of horseflesh in the territory, I reckon," Lister said.

"Damn it, man, I'm in a hurry. How much?"

"Call it a hundred even, an' I'll throw in a saddle and bridle."

"The horse isn't worth but forty."

"Take it or leave it. I'm not the one that's afoot."

Drake was beat and he knew it.

He'd taken Helen Lee's money and promised to keep her safe. Now, for some reason, she'd chosen to put herself in harm's way. He owed it to her to at least make an effort to find her.

Besides, Lister was right. One day he may need a fast horse.

"Saddle him for me," Drake said.

Lister raised his good arm and made a rubbing motion with his thumb and forefinger.

Drake paid him.

"Lister," he said, "you'll end up getting hung."

The old man cackled. "Maybe you an' me together, sonny."

Lister saddled the sorrel and handed Drake the reins. "Slicker on the nail over there by the door," he said. "She'll keep you dry 'cept where she's got holes."

The slicker was stiff and cracked and smelled of

horseshit. But Drake shrugged into it, then mounted the sorrel.

"Be careful," Lister said. "It ain't a mornin' for riding."

As he rode into the wind and teeming rain, Drake considered that.

Why would Helen Lee ride out on a day like this?

He had no answer.

Drake rode west along the bank of a twisting creek. To the north the eighteen-hundred-foot peaks of the Sans Bois Mountains were shrouded in cloud and rain; the oak, pine, and hickory forests covering their slopes were dark green, dripping wet.

Thunder roiled the black sky and white pools of lightning flared inside the clouds, alarming the sorrel, who tossed his head, jangling the bit.

Drake rode for thirty minutes, head bent against the downpour, then pulled into the shelter of a stand of hardwoods.

Blowing rain cartwheeling around him, he built a cigarette and burned up half a dozen matches before finally getting it lit.

The vast land stretched away in all directions. Nothing moved but the rippling bluestem grass, the only sound the sigh of the wind and the snake hiss of the rain.

The butt of Drake's cigarette sizzled into the grass and he prepared to move out. He planned on going back to town. Finding Helen Lee in this wilderness was wellnigh impossible.

But a few moments later he saw her. And she was not alone.

The woman was wearing a yellow slicker and a man's

hat, but even at a distance, the red fire of her hair was unmistakable. She rode at a canter in the direction of town, a tall man on a buckskin horse keeping pace with her.

Drake had seen that horse before, outside the Bon-Ton Hotel. It belonged to the man named Henry.

Lovers go riding together, Drake told himself. Nothing too unusual in that. But they don't do it in the middle of a goddamned tempest.

His first inclination was to go after them, but he dismissed that idea as quickly as it had formed.

Best to follow their back trail and discover where they'd been and why. The why of the thing must have been mighty important to Helen Lee for her to ride all the way out here in a storm.

Drake glanced at the leaden sky, a frown of doubt wrinkling the corners of his eyes.

Why the hell was he doing this?

The woman was safe and his search had justified the wages she was paying him.

But, like the pain from a returning toothache, he suddenly knew why.

The fragment of conversation he'd heard in the early-morning hours came back to him.

Helen Lee's voice.

". . . expendable . . . idiot . . ."

Drake knew she'd been talking about him. And it rankled.

Did she mean to use him for a while, then have Henry kill him?

The answer could lie back there among the foothills of the Sans Bois, and Chauncey Drake intended to find it.

Chapter 11

The passage of two horses had scarred the bluestem and Drake followed the tracks west.

After a mile the riders had swung to the northeast through shallow, rolling hills, some crested by thin stands of pine and hardwood.

Drake lost the trail on a stretch where the soil had been blown away by generations of wind to the hardpan.

But he saw where Helen Lee had likely been headed.

A shallow creek lay in front of him, pocked by rain, beyond that a cabin and outbuildings, then the craggy peak of Little Yancy Mountain, slabs of sandstone jutting through its thick covering of pine and hickory.

Drake splashed across the creek, then drew rein on the sorrel. His eyes scanned the cabin and barn, but detected no movement.

It was a raw, rainy day, and smoke should have been rising from the cabin chimney, but there was none. One of the barn doors was shut, the other yawned open.

Drake kneed the sorrel forward.

A sixty-foot hackberry shaded the cabin, and wild-flowers grew in white and blue painted boxes under its windows.

A woman was living here.

Or had been.

Suspicion lay heavy on Drake and instinctively his hand moved to the Colt under his slicker.

He stood in the stirrups. "Hello, the house!"

The cabin turned blank eyes to Drake and the hack-berry stirred uneasily in the wind, whispering. Rain beat around him, drumming on the domed crown of his plug hat.

Drake rode to the cabin and swung out of the saddle. Something on the muddy ground caught his eye and he bent to look.

Wheel tracks, made recently, stretched away from him, narrowing to a gradual vee before disappearing from sight between a pair of hills.

But no farm wagon, even one heavily loaded, had made these tracks.

The wheels were at least six inches wide and had sunk deeply into the mud. A cannon might have made these tracks, and a mighty big one at that.

It occurred to Drake that the cabin looked as though it had once been a warm, welcoming place, but now, silent and still, it was a thing of menace.

He swallowed hard, the reins in his hands, hardly daring to move.

Years before, when he was fourteen, Drake had gone up the Goodnight-Loving Trail, and he still had the cowboy's superstitious dread of ha'ants and such.

He was convinced this was the farm where Stella Waters had met her terrible end.

What had Helen Lee been doing here?

"Mr. Waters!" Drake yelled. "Jim Waters!"

"Call all you like. He ain't coming."

His already tense nerves clamoring, Drake swung around, hand clawing for his Colt.

"I wouldn't, mister. I got me a Greener scattergun."

A small, compact man with a spade-shaped beard regarded Drake with mild blue eyes. But there was nothing mild about the shotgun he held rock steady in his hands.

"Damn it, you scared the hell out of me," Drake said.

"I do that to folks sometimes," the small man said.

"Where's Waters?"

"Dead."

"You kill him?"

"Nope."

"Then who did?"

"I don't know for sure."

Thinking of Helen Lee, Drake said, "Lay a guess on me."

"I'm not a guessing man. When I know who killed Waters I'll say it clear enough."

Drake studied the little man. He was of early middle age and didn't look like an outlaw, but he didn't look like a lawman either. He wore a bowler hat and under his rain-soaked slicker showed the lapels of a black, high-button broadcloth suit, a celluloid collar, and blue-and-gold striped tie. He could have been a bank clerk, or a preacher.

The man read Drake's eyes and smiled.

"My name is Reuben Withers. I'm a Pinkerton agent."

"You mean, like a detective?"

"Yes, like a detective."

"Who do you work for?" Drake was suspicious and wary. "Helen Lee?"

"No, I work in Washington for a man named Benjamin Harrison."

Drake was taken aback. "You don't mean the new president?"

Withers said, "Oh, but I do."

Deciding to leave his questions aside for now, Drake said, "They call me—"

"I know who you are, Mr. Drake. And that until recently you were incarcerated in the Green Meadow jail, convicted and condemned for the murder of a prostitute."

"I didn't kill—"

"I know you didn't." Withers lowered the Greener. "Follow me, Mr. Drake. There's something you ought to see. I discovered it when I put my horse up in the barn."

As Drake fell into step beside him, Withers turned his head and said, "Do you have a strong stomach, Mr. Drake?"

"I guess so. Why?"

"You're going to need it."

Chapter 12

They walked to the barn under a lowering sky, splashing through mud puddles, hammered by a spiraling rain. Lightning scrawled its calling card and violent thunder blasted the clouds apart.

"Prepare yourself," Withers said when they reached the open door of the barn.

It was dark inside and it took Drake's eyes a few moments to become accustomed to the gloom.

Then he saw what Withers had seen.

"Oh, my God," Drake whispered.

He felt the Pinkerton's hand on his elbow. "Steady, old chap."

A man and a woman hung from a rafter, both naked, both badly abused before death. There was evidence of a beating, violent rape in the case of the woman, and someone had obviously enjoyed himself with a branding iron.

A cardboard placard on a string hung around Jim Waters's neck. It read:

GET OUT!

"Who . . ."

Drake swallowed hard and tried again.

"Who is the woman?"

"I thought you might know," Withers said.

Drake shook his head.

"Apparently she had the great misfortune to be visiting Mr. Waters when the killers struck," Withers said. "It would appear that the late Mrs. Waters wasn't her husband's only love interest."

Drake turned and stepped to the door and stood for a few moments looking out at the rain. He built a cigarette and without looking around said, "Who did this, Withers?"

"I'll tell you when I know for sure."

"Why all these killings?"

"Ah, a better question, Mr. Drake."

Drake waited long enough to light his smoke, then said, "Well?"

"I believe—this is only my opinion, mind—that for some reason this land has suddenly become more valuable than the lives of the people who live on it."

Withers extracted a long, black cheroot from a silver case and thumbed a match into flame. He lit the cigar and inhaled gratefully, then said, "Mr. Drake, have you ever heard this quote? It goes, 'The way to make money is to buy when blood is running in the streets.'"

"Can't say as I have. Who said it?"

"A man called John D. Rockefeller."

"Who is he?"

"A very rich, very powerful financier, among other things."

Something echoed in Drake's brain, but he could not bring it to mind.

"Why are you telling me this?" he said finally.

"No reason, really. But it's a quote to remember, is it not?" Withers's blue eyes were free of guile and he was smiling slightly.

Drake let the question go, and threw his cigarette butt into the rain.

"Storm or not, we've got some burying to do," he said.

Drake and Withers sat at the scrubbed pine table in the Waterses' cabin.

Withers had lit a fire in the stove and made coffee, sweetened with the Hennessy brandy he'd brought from his saddlebags.

Over the rim of his cup, Drake stared at Withers, who was industriously brushing mud from his pants.

"Why would the president send a Pinkerton to this part of the territory?" Drake said. "To head off a range war?"

Withers smiled. "Why would you say that?"

"When the land suddenly becomes valuable enough to kill for, it usually means a fight for grass."

"A good point, Mr. Drake, but it's been my experience that when cattlemen want someone else's range, they go right ahead and take it and get ready for a fight."

He shook his head. "No, it's not grass. God knows there's plenty of open range around these parts."

"Then what? Gold, maybe?"

"It's possible." Withers stopped what he was doing, sipped from his cup, then said, "But whoever is behind these murders also wants the town of Green Meadow and the land it stands on. That's why the prostitute was killed. And there will be more murders to come that I'm powerless to prevent."

Withers picked up his coat and began brushing. "I'm sure money is to be made in Green Meadow, but it's by no means a gold mine."

"It's a hick town, that's all, worth nothing."

"I know, but it may be that it's not the buildings, but the ground itself that's valuable."

"Damn it, Withers, Green Meadow sits on shale rock and cactus."

The Pinkerton smiled. "Indeed it does, Mr. Drake, indeed it does."

Withers scraped at a mud spot with his thumbnail. Without looking up from his task, he said, "I need your help, Mr. Drake."

"Why? Not that I plan on offering any."

As though he hadn't heard, Withers said, "You will help me bring down a vile, evil creature, and, in doing so, you'll save the lives of many people, including your own."

Chapter 13

Chauncey Drake rose, crossed to the stove, and poured himself more coffee. He returned to the table, added a shot of brandy, and built, then lit, a cigarette before speaking.

"Withers," he said finally, "I'm working for a woman named Helen Lee. Once she pays me the rest of the money she promised, I'm drifting out of this territory and I ain't never coming back."

The Pinkerton cast a fastidious eye over his coat, then laid it carefully on the table.

Behind a cloud of cigar smoke, he said, "Helen Lee, real name Mary Jane Mackinac, sometimes goes by the alias Catherine Mundy. Born Cork, Ireland, date of birth unknown. In 1886 Lee spent six months in the Essex County Jail, New Jersey, for grand larceny. Suspected of murdering an elderly gentleman in El Paso, Texas, another in Santa Fe, Arizona Territory. Travels with a small-time con artist by the name of Henry Roberts. Lee passes Roberts off as her brother. In fact, he's her common-law husband."

Withers paused for effect, then said, "Is that the Helen Lee you're talking about?"

"No. You must have a different Helen Lee," Drake said.

"Tall, slim, red hair and green eyes. A looker. A real snapper, as they say."

"Sounds like her."

"It is her."

Drake shrugged. "Listen, Pinkerton man. The lady is paying me to protect her. That's all. I don't care how the skeletons in her closet are dancing."

"Protect her from whom?"

"I don't know. Everybody, I guess."

"The Fat Man?"

"How did you . . . I mean . . ."

"If Miss Lee is trying to con the Fat Man, she'll need all the protection she can get." Withers's gaze wandered over Drake. "And, quite frankly, I don't think you cut it."

Stung, Drake thudded his cup onto the table.

"Don't worry about me, Withers. I can cut it."

"You ever hear of a man named Harvey Thornton?"

"Sure, everybody has. He's a gunfighter out of Laredo."

"Good, would you say?"

"The best there is. He's killed seven men."

"Many more than that, Mr. Drake. Thornton works for the Fat Man." A smile tugged at Withers's mouth. "Still think you can cut it?"

Suddenly angry, more out of fear than irritation, Drake said, "Damn it, who is this Fat Man I keep hearing about?"

"He's a man who takes what he wants—land, banks, railroads, ships, businesses . . . a woman. If he decides he wants Miss Lee in his stinking bed, he'll take her and mount her like a great walrus."

"Is that all he wants, Helen Lee?"

The Pinkerton shook his head. "No, that's not all. I believe he wants all the land in this part of the territory. Take Green Meadow as a center, then draw a circle around it fifty miles in all directions. That's what the Fat Man wants. And he'll kill to get it."

Drake heard rain rattling on the windows, thunder booming in the bruised sky, and the wind's wheezing intake of breath.

"All this means nothing to me, Withers," he said. "I'm leaving town."

Withers stepped to the stove and poured coffee.

When he came back he said, "The Fat Man was here. Did you see the wagon tracks outside?"

Drake nodded.

"You asked me who hanged the two people in the barn and I told you I didn't know. But I'm pretty sure the Fat Man murdered Waters and his girlfriend, probably just an hour before I got here. He didn't do it personally, but he ordered it done."

"Why, for God's sake?"

"He wants this farm. It's a small start, but it's a start. After the Fat Man had his wife murdered, Waters didn't run. Signed his own death warrant right there."

"The people in Green Meadow didn't run after Loretta Sinclair was murdered, either. Was her death the Fat Man's doing?"

"It's my belief that the whore's death was only a start. I know how the Fat Man thinks. Kill enough people in Green Meadow and they'll pack up and run, abandon the town."

"But the law can stop this."

"What law? Why do you think President Harrison hired the Pinkertons? It's because he doesn't put much faith in a few overworked deputy marshals to enforce the law in nearly seventy thousand square miles of territory."

Withers's gaze drifted out the window, then back to Drake. "I'm afraid Green Meadow is on its own."

Drake nodded. "And without me."

"Is that your final word?"

"I don't owe the town a thing. They were going to hang me, remember?"

"And they still might. How are you going to explain all this?"

"All what?"

"The death of Jim Waters and his fancy woman?"

"You trying to blackmail me, Withers?"

"No, just stating a fact. If you go back and report that you found the bodies and buried them, you'll be the prime suspect."

"Again."

"Seems like I don't have to spell it out, does it?"

"I have nothing back at Green Meadow. I can keep on riding."

Withers's eyes hardened. "I can't let that happen, Mr. Drake."

The derringer came out fast, hammer back, twin muzzles steady on the bridge of Drake's nose.

"You might make it out of the territory. You might not. I can't take even the slightest risk of my true identity being revealed by you or anyone else. As far as Green Meadow knows, I'm a liquor drummer, and I have to keep it that way."

"You going to shoot me, Withers?"

"If I have to."

The Pinkerton took out his watch, thumbed it open, and laid it on the table.

Drake heard its steady *tick . . . tick . . . tick . . .*

"Mr. Drake," Withers said, "whether you live or die depends on what we say to each other over the next few minutes."

Chapter 14

Withers reached out with his left hand and jerked Drake's Colt from the holster. He opened the loading gate, held the revolver upright, and let the rounds fall out of the chambers. He scooped up the shells, dropped them in his pocket, then slid the gun back to Drake.

"Now we can talk," he said.

"Talk away," Drake said. "You're the one holding the stinger."

A lightning flash flared inside the shadowed cabin, for an instant overwhelming the ruddy glow of the stove. There was no letup in the rain and the glass panes streamed like a widow woman's tears.

"Mr. Drake, I've been sent here to bring down the Fat Man," Withers said. "There's something big being cooked up and he wants his filthy fingers in the pie."

"And what's that to me?"

"The Fat Man kills without conscience. He has murdered men, women, and children and his crooked business dealings have ruined the lives of thousands of others. He has been accused of rape, homicide, larceny, robbery, piracy on the high seas, slave trading, and treason."

"Then he should have been hanged years ago."

"Yes, he should have been, but his expensive lawyers have beaten the charges every time."

"And now President Harrison thinks you can finally nail him to the wall."

"That is the president's belief, yes."

"Withers, excuse me while I laugh." But Drake didn't laugh, he blazed anger. "Hell, man, this is the Oklahoma Territory! Outlaws walk around Green Meadow every day carrying that kind of baggage."

"No, Mr. Drake, they're not like the Fat Man. If evil is a total absence of good, free of any trace of human empathy, then he's the most evil creature on earth."

The Pinkerton sat back in his chair, but the derringer in his hand was steady. "He is also an enemy of the United States and all it stands for and holds dear. The Fat Man would replace love with hate, order with anarchy, peace with war, and civilization with barbarism and the law of the jungle."

"Why not put a bullet in his fat belly?"

"The Fat Man can't be killed."

"Any man can be killed."

"There's never been a bullet cast that has the Fat Man's name on it. I'll have to bring him down some other way."

"Withers, damn it, he's not bulletproof."

The Pinkerton took a sip of coffee before he spoke. "You saw the wheel tracks out there?"

"Yeah, I saw them. A heavy wagon, I reckon."

"Very heavy. When he's not on his train, the Fat Man travels everywhere in an armored coach that is, as you say, bulletproof. He also surrounds himself with body-guards, twenty men chosen for their gun skills."

"Like Harvey Thornton?"

"He's the best of them—or the worst, depending on how you look at it."

Drake smiled. "All that, and you want me to throw in with you?"

"I'm not asking it for me, Mr. Drake. I'm asking you to do it for your country."

"You're appealing to my patriotism?"

"You could say that."

Drake was silent for a few moments. Then he said, "If I say, 'No, I'm riding,' you'll kill me."

"Yes."

Withers's eyes were bleak, resigned, like a man who has decided on a course of action and will stick with it, no matter what.

"You don't give me much choice," Drake said.

"Live or die, Mr. Drake. It's simple."

The knuckle of the Pinkerton's trigger finger was white

"All right, I'll be a patriot, a regular little George Washington."

Withers did not smile. "Just don't turn out to be a Benedict Arnold, Mr. Drake."

Thunder crashed.

Then the glass in the window shattered.

And Reuben Withers was blown out of his chair.

Chapter 15

Withers was sprawled on his back on the floor.

As another bullet smashed through the window and whined viciously off the iron stove, Drake threw the table aside and ducked behind the window.

He looked at the Pinkerton.

The man had a bad cut across his forehead, but the scarlet splash of blood on his right shoulder spoke of a more severe wound.

Drake removed the five .44-40 shells from Withers's pocket and reloaded his Colt. He hammered two fast shots out the window, firing at rain and wind.

Withers stirred and groaned.

Drake knelt beside him.

It looked like the bushwhacker's bullet had entered the meat of the man's right shoulder, ranged upward, then exited at his collarbone before burning across his forehead.

"Wha-what's happening?" the Pinkerton asked.

"We're deep in it. That's what's happening," Drake said.

A bullet slammed into the cabin, then another.

"Somebody's trying to kill you, Withers, or me, or both of us."

The Pinkerton groggily rose to a sitting position, but Drake pushed him back to the floor. "Keep your damn fool head down or you'll get it blowed off."

Withers's hand went to his shoulder and came away glistening red. "I'm shot."

Drake nodded. "They really teach you Pinkerton dicks to use your powers of observation, don't they?"

"But . . . but who?"

"Maybe you sold somebody bad booze, Withers."

Drake raised his head and glanced out the window. A curtain blew across his face and he jerked it onto the floor.

Through a turbulent storm of wind and rain, he scanned the creek. A single cottonwood stood on the bank to his left. On the opposite bank a tangle of sandstone slabs spiked out of the earth.

The shots could have come from either place . . . or a dozen others.

A dry shuffling drew Drake's attention.

He turned and saw Withers drag himself across the floor to the corner where he'd propped his shotgun.

A smear of blood followed him, like the track of a gut-shot snail.

Withers struggled to a sitting position, his back against the wall, and he laid the Greener across his thighs.

"Stay at the window, Mr. Drake," he said. "I've got the door covered."

Drake turned away and smiled. The little man had sand.

His smile slipped as he realized something else. Withers really would have shot him. There was no doubt about that.

Minutes passed and there were no more shots.

Crouching low, Drake made his way to Withers's side.

"My shoulder feels bad," the Pinkerton said.

"It is bad. You're shot through and through."

"Damn it. I didn't need this, not now."

"Bullets can be downright inconvenient," Drake said. He examined Withers's shoulder. "You're losing blood. I have to get you to a doctor."

"It was a hunting accident, Mr. Drake. Remember that."

Irritated, Drake said, "Withers, don't you think that the ranny who shot you is aware of your true identity?"

"Yes, but the fewer other people who know, the better. I must come and go as I please in Green Meadow."

"Suit yourself. So, I was aiming at a deer and plugged you by mistake. How's that sound?"

"About right, I'd say."

"I'm going out there to take a look-see. If the coast is clear, I'll bring your horse and we'll skedaddle."

He handed Withers his Colt.

"Take this and give me the Greener. I'm not real handy with Sammy's gun unless I'm up close."

"Be careful, Mr. Drake."

"You can count on that, Mr. Withers."

Chapter 16

Drake ducked through the cabin door, then sprinted for the corner. He got down on one knee and studied the land around the creek.

A rising wind tore at him and rain pounded him relentlessly.

Out there in the dusky day there was no sign of life. Wind stirred the branches of the cottonwood and the creek rippled, splashing over its banks.

Drake rose and walked toward the tree, his heart pounding in his ears.

"Goddamn it!"

A jackrabbit rose out of nowhere and got tangled in Drake's feet before bounding away.

His nerves jangling, Drake aired out his lungs, cursing after the rabbit and the mother that bore him.

Then it dawned on him that he hadn't attracted a bullet. The bushwhacker must be long gone.

The dirt and sand around the cottonwood was undisturbed. He splashed across the creek and walked to the rocks, the scattergun across his chest.

Behind a broken slab he saw footprints, a couple of cigarette butts, and several shell casings. Drake picked one of them up. Fifty caliber, a killing round.

He stood and his eyes moved along the foothills of the Sans Bois and he saw nothing but the wind and rain.

"Tall man, around two hundred pounds, dresses like a drover but wears boots no puncher could afford. And he's left-handed."

Withers stepped beside Drake. He had wrapped the torn-down curtain around his shoulder. It was already glistening with blood.

"You shouldn't be out there," Drake said. "You'll bleed to death."

"Heard you hollering and came to investigate."

"I got spooked."

"By the gunman?"

"No, by a rabbit."

"Ah, must have been a real ferocious one, huh?"

Drake gave Withers a sidelong glance, but the man's face was empty.

The Pinkerton took the shell casing from Drake's hand.

"From a Sharps .50, I'd say." He nodded to the ground. "See the boot prints? High heels, a well-cut sole, and in new condition. If he was a working drover, his boots would be badly worn. Judging by the depth of the prints, he's a big man, around two hundred pounds."

Withers studied more tracks. "Wide step. I'd guess he's well over six feet."

"And left-handed?"

The Pinkerton took a small magnifying glass from his pocket and studied the broken rock slab.

After a few moments he straightened and said, "He leaned his rifle in that narrow crevice in the rock. Scraped the sandstone a little with the barrel. He knelt, but the indent of his knee is to the right of the crevice, and that suggests he was shooting off his left shoulder."

"Harvey Thornton draws with his left hand," Drake said. "I read that somewhere."

"It might well have been him."

"So the Fat Man knows who and what you are."

"Yes, and he knows why I'm here."

Drake was concerned about Withers. The little man was very pale and he swayed on his feet. Pink blood mixed with rain ran down his arm and over his hand.

But he had to ask the question.

"I thought only the president knows why you're here."

Withers smiled slightly. "Mr. Drake, there are no secrets in Washington, and the Fat Man has spies everywhere."

"Well, hell, where do we go from here?"

"A doctor's office, I'd say."

"I meant, after that."

"I don't think we're calling the shots anymore, Mr. Drake. I believe our enemies will come to us."

Drake didn't like that "our enemies."

He didn't like that at all.

Dr. John Rosewell was young and earnest, and lectured Drake on the careless discharge of firearms. The good news was that the bullet had gone through Withers clean and had not broken any bones.

He disinfected the Pinkerton's wounds, stitched him

up, and gave him something for pain. Finally he said that Withers's chest was a tad wheezy, that that was worrisome, and ordered him to give up cigars and ardent spirits.

"Rest that shoulder for a couple of weeks, then come back and see me," the physician said. "If you detect a smell of rotten meat from the wound, come back at once."

Withers stood under Sy Goldberg's canvas awning and lit a cigar. Beside him, Drake watched the rain and planned his escape.

Goldberg glared at the two men from behind his steamed-up window. He had never quite figured out how to charge people for sheltering under his awning, but he was working on it.

"Well, Mr. Withers," Drake said, "I'm glad I could be of help. Now I got to be moving on."

The Pinkerton smiled, but did not turn his head.

"You won't get far, Mr. Drake," he said.

"You'll come after me? With a busted shoulder?"

"No, the Fat Man will do that for me."

"Want to add anything to that last remark?" Drake said, irritated.

"Only this: The man who tried to kill me knew there were two men in the cabin, and that one was me, the other you. Now the Fat Man thinks you know what I know, and he'll try to destroy you."

Withers turned, still smiling. "Ride away, Mr. Drake, by all means. See how far you get."

Drake felt like a trapped animal. He stood silent, numb, studying the angles, searching for a way out. He found none. He was stuck to Withers, joined at the hip, like the twins from Siam he'd once seen in a carnival sideshow.

And he owed Helen Lee money that he could not pay back. She might come looking for him, too.

"Friends of yours coming, Mr. Drake?" Withers asked.

Drake followed his gaze and saw Marshal Dub Halloran stomping toward them along the boardwalk. Three riders kept pace with him along the rain-swept street, their horses kicking up spurts of mud.

The lawman's face was black with anger and as he got closer he cleared his slicker from his gun.

Nothing about this, Drake told himself, bodes well.

Chapter 17

"Chauncey Drake! Don't run from me!"

"I wasn't about to run anywhere, Dub," Drake said.

"You son of a bitch, you're the baddest man in the territory," Halloran said.

Suddenly his Remington was up, hammer back, leveled at Drake's head.

"Are these the men?"

"That's them, Marshal. We seen 'em plain."

The rider who had spoken attracted Drake's attention.

Judging by the man's face, he lived in a cave. His mouth was wide, thick-lipped, bulging over thick canine teeth, and a massive brow ridge, tufted with spikes of coarse hair, overhung sunken eyes.

One sunken eye.

The other was gone, scarred by a vertical knife cut. But the man had tattooed an eye over the puckered skin that covered the socket. Stark white with a jet-black pupil. Staring. Unmoving. Malevolent.

"Seen them two bury Jim Waters and a woman."

"You tell him, Harvey," a young towheaded rider said.

"Them folks was naked," the man called Harvey said. "Seen them two point and laugh at the woman's shame as they was throwing her in the grave."

Anger flared in Drake. He looked at the horseman. "You're a damned liar," he said.

"He's callin' you out, Mr. Thornton," the towhead grinned.

Harvey Thornton stiffened in the saddle, his good eye icing. He was a man who had killed before and was eager to kill again.

Halloran stopped it.

"Nobody's callin' nobody out," he said. "These men are my prisoners."

He stepped to Drake, reached inside his slicker, and removed his gun. He stuck the Colt in his waistband, then relieved Withers of his derringer.

Halloran looked at Drake. "What's the name of your accomplice?"

"He can speak for himself, Dub," Drake said.

"So you can speak," the marshal said to Withers. "Then speak. What's your name?"

"John Smith."

"And wounded, I see. Jim Waters had sand and put up a fight, huh, Mr. Smith?"

Halloran motioned with his gun. "All right, Mr. Smith, follow Chauncey into my office. I see any fancy moves, I hear any sass, I'll put a bullet in both of you."

"Marshal, we done here?"

This from Harvey Thornton.

"For now. Come into town tomorrow and I'll take statements from the three of you."

"Always willing to help the law." Thornton touched his hat. "I'll be seeing you, Marshal."

Drake stopped at the office door.

"Dub, you know who that is?"

"Yeah, his name is Harvey Thornton. What of it?"

"You've never heard the name before?"

"Nah, can't say as I have."

Withers spoke to Drake. "The marshal has obviously led a sheltered life." Then to Halloran, "Harvey Thornton is a gunman-for-hire, a fast-draw artist and contract killer. He'll cut any man, woman, or child in half with a shotgun for fifty dollars."

"So you say." The marshal smirked.

"So I know."

"Mr. Smith, you're a bigger liar than your friend Chauncey. Now get in there before I bend this hogleg over your thick skull."

"Why didn't you tell him you were a Pinkerton?"

"If I had, he wouldn't have believed me. And even if he did, it wouldn't have made any difference."

Withers shrugged. "Halloran left town with a posse. I'd guess they've dug up the bodies by this time."

"They'll hang us, you know," Drake said. "Depend on it."

Withers stood with his back against the cell bars, a small man with slumped shoulders and a resigned expression on his face.

"Seems like," he said.

"Damn it, have Halloran wire the president. He'll help."

"No, he won't. He told me if this went wrong, he'd

wash his hands of the whole affair. I told you that the Fat Man has friends in Washington."

"A killer and a robber?"

"Money talks loud, Mr. Drake, and it doesn't have the Fat Man's stink on it. Ever smelled a double eagle?"

Drake watched a smile grow on Withers's face. "Say it," the Pinkerton told him.

"How long have we got?"

"Not long. The Fat Man wants rid of us. He thinks we got too close."

"Close to what, damn it? I know nothing about him."

"Too close to the reason for his being here in Green Meadow."

"And what is the reason?"

"I don't know."

Drake threw up his hands in frustration. "Nobody knows anything."

Withers's smile blossomed into a laugh.

"Only the Fat Man knows," he said.

Chapter 18

The remainder of the day dragged past, darkened to a rain-racked night, then to a dull, watery dawn.

At eight, Halloran brought coffee, bacon, beans, and a loaf of sourdough bread.

"Eat hearty, boys," he said, "I won't have time to bring supper."

"Trying to save money on the prisoners' grub?" Drake asked.

"Hell no, I do that anyway."

The marshal paused for effect, then said, "Mr. John D. Rockefeller, the millionaire, is holding a town meeting in Sy Goldberg's store tonight." He puffed up a little. "Of course, I was asked to attend."

Suddenly Withers was interested.

"A meeting about what?"

"He wants to buy the town, lock, stock, and barrel, and all the ranches and farms around it. And he's prepared to offer top dollar, I'm told."

"Why?" Drake asked.

"I don't know." Halloran scowled. "Here, that's none

of your damned business, Chauncey. All you've done is cost this town money. Right now them meat hogs are stinking up Sy's store pretty bad."

"Marshal Halloran," Withers said, trying to sound fawning and succeeding, "I can understand why the town would want you to be there. Mr. Rockefeller is a very important man and needs guarding."

"Damn right," the marshal said, smiling, the flattery bending him a little.

"Is he alone? I mean, did he bring an entourage?"

"I don't know what an ent-enter—whatever that damned word means, but he's not by himself. He's brought a friend, a German by the name of Karl Benz. Seems like he'd invented a horseless carriage that Mr. Rockefeller is interested in buying."

Halloran laughed, then said, "Well, that's what Sy Goldberg says, but I don't believe him. Whoever heard of a carriage that moves without a horse?"

"Indeed, Marshal," Withers said. "Sounds like nonsense to me."

Halloran grunted and motioned to the food tray. "Slide that under the bars when you're done. Helps keep the rats down in the cell."

He started to walk away, then stopped and turned. "By the way, we dug them bodies up." Halloran's smile was unpleasant. "You boys will be fitted for a pine box real soon."

After the marshal left, Withers was silent for a long time, staring at nothing, his chin propped on his right fist. A pulse beat steadily in his forehead.

The rain had stopped briefly, but it was now drizzling again and watered-down daylight formed triangles of shadow in the corners of the cell where the rats and spiders lived.

Drake was not an outdoorsman. He was a creature of the saloons, but, like Withers, he was deep in thought, his mind miles away, lost somewhere in the Sans Bois Mountains.

He was sitting in a sheltered spot, under ticking pines, a smoking coffeepot on the fire, watching the rain come down.

Withers's voice dragged him back to the present place and time.

"You know what makes men like John D. Rockefeller different from the rest of us, Mr. Drake?"

"Money."

"Yes, money. And the reasons they have for acquiring that money. Men like Rockefeller don't plan a week ahead, or a month or a year, like the rest of us. They plan for decades hence, for the establishment of dynasties."

"Very interesting, Withers, but what's that got to do with us getting hung?"

"Indirectly, everything."

"Then roll it out."

"The day of the horseless carriage is coming sooner than we think, Mr. Drake."

"Damn it, Withers, I've never known a man that talks in circles the way you do."

"Rockefeller is president of Standard Oil. The last I heard, the company was worth two hundred million dollars, with a working capital of seventy million."

"Big money."

"You're right, big money. Now Rockefeller's here with his friend Karl Benz." Withers's small frame looked translucent in the gauzy morning light. "What does Benz manufacture?"

"Horseless carriages. Hell, you told me that already."

"And what will Benz's horseless carriages use for fuel?"

"Steam?"

"Petroleum. Now do you see the connection?"

Drake shook his head. "I don't know what petroleum is, Withers. And neither does anybody else."

"It's made from oil, Mr. Drake, and Rockefeller has a monopoly on all the oil produced in this country, currently twenty million barrels a year. Fifteen, twenty years from now if Rockefeller and Benz have their way and the mass-produced horseless carriage becomes a reality, they estimate a consumption of five hundred million barrels."

Drake forked up the last of his greasy bacon, his face blank.

Undeterred, Withers said, "I believe this land could be swimming in oil and that's why it's suddenly become so valuable. Rockefeller wants it all, from the Sans Bois south to the Kiamichi Mountains, east and west as far as the eye can see, and farther."

Despite himself, Drake was interested. "And that's what the meeting tonight is all about—oil."

"Yes, only Rockefeller won't tip his hand. As far as the rubes in Green Meadow are concerned, he wants farmland."

"So he's behind all the killings, including the two they've pinned on us."

Withers tossed his fork on his plate and made a face. "That damned marshal should be shot, feeding us this swill."

He looked at Drake, his eyes shadowed, like holes burned in paper.

"John D. Rockefeller won't have anything to do with murder. But he was willing to stand aside and let the Fat Man try it his way, and it didn't work. So now he'll do it his own way and buy the land at a fraction of its potential worth."

"If he does that, what's in it for the Fat Man?"

"A finder's fee. He'll work his own angle."

"Will the townspeople and the farms and ranchers sell?"

"I don't know. If they don't, Rockefeller will go back to New York or wherever it is he goes, and let the Fat Man work it out. That will mean killing, a lot more killing. He'll terrorize this country and force the people out."

"That will leave us in the clear," Drake said.

"Don't count on it. The Fat Man wants us dead. He tried to kill us at the Waters place, and when that failed, he got his boys to sell us down the river."

Withers smiled. "And Halloran didn't need much convincing. The town is still pretty upset about those meat hogs."

Chapter 19

The day shaded into night. The rain had stopped, but the wind had picked up, making every loose door and store sign in town creak and bang.

"Last time I was here, I had a little cat visit me," Drake said, talking into darkness.

"Oh, yeah?" Withers said.

"Yeah, little calico cat."

"Did it bring a mouse?"

"Nah, just came by itself."

"I like cats. Little kittlin' cats."

"Me too."

A silence stretched between them; then Drake said, "Ever own a cat?"

"No, I never did. They make good pets, though. I heard that."

The front door slammed open and booted feet pounded on the office floor.

"Damn it," Drake said, his eyes wide, "vigilantes."

He rose to his feet, determined to sell his life dear.

Harvey Thornton loomed at the bars, two others with him.

"Hurry," he said, "you two are coming with us."

A key clanked and the door swung open.

Drake clenched his fists. "Thornton, you ain't putting a hemp necktie on me."

"We're getting out of here," the gunman said. "Hell, I'm saving your fool neck, not breaking it."

Thornton's Colt waved Withers to the door. "You, out. We've got horses waiting outside."

"Best offer I've had today," the Pinkerton said.

He stepped after Thornton and Drake followed.

Thornton stopped them just inside the office door. He walked outside, looked up and down the street, then beckoned them forward.

"I don't want to gun that idiot marshal," he said. "At least not yet."

Drake and Withers swung into the saddle and Thornton led his cavalcade out of town.

"Where are you taking us?" Drake asked.

"To meet a friend of yours."

"Who?"

"The Fat Man," Thornton said. He grinned. "I hope you don't puke real easy."

They rode west through gathering darkness, threading their way among rocks and stunted juniper as they took a trail closer to the foothills of the Sans Bois.

The dank wind tore at them, and Drake pulled his plug hat down over his ears as he fought to keep it on his head.

After crossing Rock Creek, Thornton swung north

into heavily timbered country, the invisible bulk of Little Yancy somewhere off to the east.

Drake estimated they rode three miles through a wide valley before cutting due west toward Little Round Mountain.

Thornton led the way along a rocky trail between two low hills, then drew rein as a voice called out from the darkness.

"Who goes there?"

"Thornton."

"Head on through, Harvey."

They passed the guard and rode into a clearing, bordered by thick forests of hardwood, cedar, and pine. A dozen tents were pitched around several campfires and the flickering silhouettes of armed men moved among them.

But what drew Drake's attention was a cabin that backed up to a low ridge of sandstone rock. The building was small, made of sawed white-painted timber, and it had a peaked tin roof and a smoking iron chimney. There were no windows, but lanterns glowed on each side of the door, staining the paint a dull crimson.

Two men, rifles across their chests, stood guard.

Thornton followed Drake's eyes and grinned. "See that painted line five yards in front of the cabin? That's the dead-line. Them boys have orders to shoot dead any man who crosses that line without leave."

"Friendly place," Drake said.

"Mister," Thornton said, no longer smiling, his tattooed eye grotesque in the darkness, "we ain't your friends."

The gunman motioned to Drake and Withers to dismount. They followed him to one of the tents.

"You'll bunk here," he said. "If either of you tries to escape, we'll track you down and I'll shoot all the fingers off your left hand. Try it a second time, and I'll do the same to the right."

Drake smiled, a devil in him. "What happens if there's a third time? You start on our toes?"

"There won't be a third time," Thornton said.

He told Drake and Withers they had the run of the camp and could eat with the men.

"There's always bacon and beans in the pot," he said. "Help yourself."

Before he left, he said, "And remember the dead-line. Get too close to the cabin and you're both dead men."

"Is that the Fat Man's quarters?" Withers asked.

Thornton's humorless smile was pinned back in place. "You'll find out soon enough. If I was you, I wouldn't be so damned impatient to meet him."

Chapter 20

There were two iron cots in the tent, both with horse-hair mattresses and a folded blanket. A kerosene lantern hung from the front tent pole, but there were no other furnishings.

"Downright homey, Mr. Drake," Withers said. He sat on the squealing cot. "Overall, it's been a strange evening."

"And stranger to come, I reckon," Drake said.

He stepped out of the tent and studied the cabin again.

It was obviously a prefabricated building that was assembled wherever the Fat Man decided to hang his hat.

Now that Drake had time to look more closely, he saw two wagons pulled into the trees to the right of the cabin. One was a huge Santa Fe freight, presumably used to transport the cabin and tents, the other looked like one of the new-fangled horse trolleys that had become popular in the big cities.

But this trolley was designed for roads, not rails.

The entire vehicle was armor-plated, windowless, its wide wheels as tall as a man, the iron tires gleaming firelight.

A team of six oxen grazed nearby, powerful animals that could haul enormous weights.

Withers stepped beside Drake. "That fortress on wheels is one of the reasons the Fat Man can't be killed," he said.

Drake nodded. "It would make it difficult, unless you had the odd cannon handy."

The Pinkerton rubbed his belly. "I've had nothing to eat since Marshal Halloran's swill." He nodded in the direction of a fire, where a huge blackened pot hung above the flames. "Do you care to make a trial of the bacon and beans, Mr. Drake?"

Several men standing near the fire silently stepped aside as Drake and Withers filled their plates.

The men displayed no belligerence and revealed little interest in the strangers.

Drake had seen such men before, in a dozen different towns located along the fringes of nowhere. They were men with careful eyes and still hands, holding their own counsel. But when the need arose, they could be as sudden and as deadly as striking rattlers.

Drake decided he wanted no part of them. Not then. Not ever.

Withers, perhaps less attuned to the ways of the professional gunman, smiled across the fire to a tall, loose-limbed man.

"I guess the rain will hold off, huh?" he said.

"Seems like," the man answered.

"I always enjoy the rain, but only when I'm indoors."

The gunman nodded, then turned away, and stepped to another fire.

"Making friends, I see," Drake said.

"Without much success, I'm afraid. I—"

The words died on Withers's lips. He was looking over Drake's shoulder to the rider on a lathered horse who had just galloped into camp.

The man jumped out of the saddle and yelled, "Harvey!"

Harvey Thornton stepped through his tent flap and walked to the man. "Well?" he asked.

"They turned him down flat."

"Lay it out."

The rider was slightly breathless.

"Sodbusters, ranchers, to a man they told him they wouldn't sell their land. The storekeepers followed suit. Sy Goldberg said he'd want a hundred times what Mr. Rockefeller was offering, and the rest pretty much agreed with him."

The man shrugged. "After that, the meeting broke up and Rockefeller headed back to the hotel."

Thornton smiled. "Then we start killing them."

"They'll fight, Harvey," the rider said. "A bunch of them boys wore the gray."

"Kill enough of them Rebs and they'll give up, just like they did in the war."

"Should I tell the Fat Man, Harvey?"

"I'll tell him. Go get something to eat or drink."

Thornton saw Drake and Withers hovering nearby.

He grinned. "Hear that, boys? They turned down Rockefeller's offer. Soon the Fat Man is going to make you two as famous as Frank and Jesse James."

Drake watched Thornton walk to the dead-line, where he stopped.

"It's Harvey," he called out to the guards. "I need to talk to the Fat Man."

One of the men ducked inside, then reappeared a few moments later. "Come on across, Harvey," he said. "You remember the horse dung?"

"I ain't likely to forget that," Thornton said.

After Thornton stepped into the cabin, Drake turned to Withers. "What did he mean make us famous?"

Withers shook his head. "I don't know, but I don't like the sound of it."

"Me neither," Drake said.

"You think we'll leave this camp alive, Mr. Drake?"

"Mr. Withers, I'm starting to think that we won't."

"It's worrisome," the Pinkerton said. "I'd say downright worrisome."

The rain started again.

The night passed without incident, and the next day came and went. Then, on the second afternoon of their stay in camp, two events occurred within hours that left Drake and Withers a lot more worried.

Chapter 21

The rain, as persistent and irritating as a nagging cough, drove Drake and Withers inside. They lay on their cots, listening to the downpour drum on the canvas.

Drake built a cigarette with makings Thornton had given him, not out of any goodwill, merely one smoker relating to the tobacco hunger of another.

The wind came from the west, and the conversation of two men at the cook fire drifted into the tent along with a reek of wood smoke.

"Charlie said the man jumped when the fifty hit him. Says three feet in the air, but that ain't hardly likely."

"I don't know. A hit with a fifty can lift a man."

"The woman just fell down right there on the board-walk. Got it right between her tits."

"Was she kicking?"

"No. Dead when she hit the timber, Charlie says."

"How many is that, Jake?"

"Just three. Them two in town and a sodbuster down by Red Oak Ridge."

"We'll be expected to make a contribution soon, I reckon."

"I'd guess."

"I don't mind killing a sodbuster. Never did like them."

"How 'bout his missus and young 'uns?"

"That's what the Fat Man is paying me for. When he stops paying, well, then . . ."

The voices faded as the men moved away.

Drake lay on his back, stunned, the cigarette burning down between his fingers.

The voices of the two gunmen had been clinical, detached, professional killers discussing the vagaries of their trade. They had betrayed neither malice nor a shred of compassion, only a keen interest on the killing power of the .50 caliber round and its effect on the human body.

Withers lay still, staring at the tent's canvas peak, as though he hadn't heard.

But then he turned his head, looked at Drake, and said, "The killing's begun, Mr. Drake."

"How the hell does the Fat Man expect to get away with this?"

"I have a feeling we're his insurance policy," Mr. Drake.

"You mean, he's using us as hostages?"

"Only to fortune, Mr. Drake, only to fortune."

Two hours later Helen Lee and Henry Roberts rode into camp.

Drake held back the tent flap and watched Helen dismount. She wore a yellow oilskin slicker over a split riding skirt, shirt, and boots, a battered hat on her head.

Her hair was soaked, lying over her shoulders in vivid auburn tendrils, her face flushed from rain and wind.

Only a truly beautiful woman could look as she did after riding through a storm. And she was all of that, Drake decided, a truly beautiful woman.

As a man took the woman's horse, Thornton emerged from his tent.

"Harvey," she said, "I need to see the Fat Man."

"He knows what happened in town, Helen. It's old news."

"Thornton, the killing has to stop. It's bad for business." This from Henry Roberts. Like Helen Lee, he wore a slicker and his gun was out of sight and unhandy.

"You trying to tell me my business, Henry?" Thornton said, low, soft, and dangerous.

"Damn it, get the Fat Man to end this killing. A respectable husband and wife gunned down in the street, another farmer . . . We'll have a U.S. marshal or the army down on us if this keeps up."

"The Fat Man told us, 'Bathe your bullets in blood, lads,' and that's what we're doing until he orders it otherwise," Thornton said.

"Harvey, we can try it my way first," Helen Lee said.

"You got more money than John D. Rockefeller? Because that's what it's going to take."

"You know I don't, but I think I can convince some of the small, hardscrabble farmers to sell to me." Helen shook her head. "No, I don't think I can. I know I can."

"The Fat Man wants it all."

"But it will be a start. We can take over the rest from there."

"You can talk to him, Helen," Thornton said. "But I warn you, he won't like it."

The woman said nothing. She was staring over Thornton's shoulder.

"What the hell is he doing here?"

The gunman turned. "Drake? He's insurance, him and his partner."

"He's useless, a waste of time. Get rid of him."

Roberts grinned, pushing back his slicker. "Want me to do it, Helen?"

But Thornton would allow himself to be pushed only so far.

"Henry, I see you go near Drake, I'll kill you."

Roberts was good with a gun, better than most on the draw and shoot, but he knew that on his best day he couldn't match Harvey Thornton. He backed off quickly. "A joke, Harvey. Just a joke."

Thornton let the man squirm for a few moments, then gave him an out.

"Later, Henry. You can gun him later."

Helen stepped into the silence that followed.

"Well, Harvey, can I talk to the Fat Man?"

"Yeah, I'll arrange it."

"When?"

"Me? Today. As for the Fat Man, he'll see you when he feels like it."

Roberts was still smarting from Thornton's unanswered challenge.

"He's a pig, a goddamned stinking hog," he said.

Thornton smiled. "Why don't you go tell him that, Henry?"

Chapter 22

Thornton showed Helen Lee and Roberts to their quarters.

A few moments later she stepped outside and braved the rain to walk to Drake's tent. Without announcing her presence, she lifted the flap and stepped inside.

Drake and Withers rose to their feet, bending at the waist because of the slope of the canvas.

"Sit, for God's sake," she said.

The woman waited until the men were seated; then she said, pink flaring on her cheekbones, "Chauncey Drake, you're a sorry piece of trash."

"It saddens me that you feel that way, Miss Lee," Drake said.

"You took my money, then ran out on me."

"I didn't run out on you. Damn it, when I couldn't find you at the hotel, I went looking for you, all the way to the Waters farm on Rock Creek."

Helen stiffened. Her eyes were accusing, locked on Drake's. "Are you implying that I had something to do with those murders?"

"I saw you and Henry ride toward the farm, then saw you ride back. That's all I'm saying."

"We saw the Fat Man's wagon outside the cabin. Jim Waters and his whore were already being killed, so we left in a hurry."

"Why were you there, Miss Lee?" Withers asked.

"Waters wanted out. He was ready to sell and I was going to make him an offer. The Fat Man had other ideas."

She looked as though she'd suddenly become aware that the question had come from Withers.

"Who the hell are you?"

"My name is Reuben Withers. I'm a friend of Mr. Drake's."

"You should be ashamed of the company you keep."

Withers smiled, but said nothing.

"You've got blood on your shirt," the woman said.

Her face showed a sudden concern that Drake figured shouldn't be there and for some reason that troubled him, but he could not figure why.

"A shoulder wound," Withers said. "The blood is seeping through the bandages, making it look worse than it is."

"Let me take a look."

"It's fine, dear lady, I assure you."

"I may need you later, in one piece. Now unbutton your shirt."

Bowing to the inevitable, Withers removed his shirt.

Helen unwound the bandages, spattering droplets of blood around the tent. She studied the shoulder, and after a while said, "The wounds are clean. Still raw, but clean."

"Thank you," Withers said. He picked up his shirt.

"Stay right there. I'll be back," the woman said.

Helen Lee returned a couple of minutes later with a handful of bandages. "You owe me a shirt, mister," she said.

After his shoulder was rebound, the Pinkerton thanked the woman, then added, "You said you may need me later. But Mr. Drake and I are prisoners here. I'm afraid there's nothing we can do to help you."

Helen stood. "If I can convince the Fat Man to stop this madness, I may not need your help."

"Rockefeller tried, and failed," Drake said.

"Maybe he didn't offer enough."

"You have more money than Standard Oil?"

Helen Lee's silence was eloquent.

Drake smiled. "Ah, then, maybe you have."

"That is none of your concern."

The woman turned to leave, but Drake's voice stopped her.

"You said if things go bad, I wasn't to let you fall into the clutches of the Fat Man. Is this the day?"

Helen Lee said nothing, but her eyes flickered, telegraphing fear she'd kept hidden until now.

From his vantage point at the tent flap, Drake watched the camp over the next couple of days. The Fat Man had still not seen fit to grant Helen Lee an audience.

Riders were constantly entering or leaving the clearing, sometimes in pairs, a few times in parties of half a dozen or more.

Then, on the afternoon of the third day, Drake and Withers witnessed an act of wanton cruelty that froze them to the bone. After it was over, they had no illusions about their survival—they were walking dead men.

Thornton and two of his gunmen dragged an old-timer into camp. The graybeard, dressed in farmer's overalls, aired out his lungs, cussing the three riders with every profanity in the book, and a few he'd made up himself.

Thornton yanked on the rope looped around the old man's neck and jerked him to the ground.

A crowd had gathered and men laughed.

"You cheap, two-bit tinhorns," the oldster bellowed, "bushwhacking an old, blind man."

Even from a distance, Drake saw that the man's eyes were full of milk. He looked to be eighty years old.

Thornton and his riders dismounted and began to tease the oldster unmercifully, kicking his butt, slapping his bearded cheeks, then ducking out of the way when the old man swung at them.

Laughter rang around the clearing, mingled with the old-timer's curses.

"Over here, Grandpa!"

"No, Pops, over here!"

The old man was game. His fists swinging, he advanced on the sound of a voice, missing with every wild punch.

"All right, I've seen enough," Drake said. "I'm going to stop this."

Withers pulled him back. "He's already dead, and there's not a thing you can do about it. You'd only get yourself killed."

Thornton and the others were getting bored with the game, but one of his men upped the ante.

"Hey, Harvey, let's give him a gun."

Thornton's face lit up, his tattooed eye fixed and staring. He called over to the guards stationed outside the Fat Man's quarters.

"You two, tell the boss to open his door if he wants to see some fun."

A man ducked inside, then reappeared. "Bring the old coot out front where he can see him, Harvey."

Thornton picked up the rope and dragged the old-ster closer to the cabin. Its door was open, but the interior was lost in darkness.

The big gunman drew his Colt and thumbed a round into the empty chamber.

"I'm giving you a gun, Pops," Thornton said. "Now you can get even."

He slapped the revolver into the old man's hand, pushed him down, then scampered out of the way.

The oldster got to his feet, his blind eyes seeing nothing, but with a terrible anger in them.

"I'm going to kill every one of you sons of bitches!" he yelled. "This is for my boy and his wife and the kids you slaughtered."

"Over here, Pops!" Thornton yelled. He moved around constantly, being careful not to stand around too long in one place.

The old man had his back to the cabin. He held the gun in both hands and cut loose.

"You missed, Pops!" a man said. "Over here!"

Another shot. Another miss.

Out by the fires, men had flattened on the ground to avoid the wild bullets.

"Over here, you old coot!"

A shot.

"Nah, old man, this way!"

A shot.

Tears were streaming down the oldster's cheeks. He knew he was missing. Knew it was hopeless.

"Over here, Pops!" Thornton said again.

Two more shots and the gun ran dry.

Thornton moved to the old man's left. "This way, Pops, take a swing at me."

The old-timer staggered forward, following the sound of Thornton's voice.

"No, this way, Pops. To your left, step to your left."

"You son of a bitch!"

The old man threw the gun at Thornton. Missed him by several feet.

"I'm to your left, you loco old fool," Thornton said. He had laughter in his voice. "Left! Left! Damn it, left!"

The old man's foot brushed the edge of the dead-line. The guards at the cabin door raised their rifles.

"A little bit more, Pops," Thornton yelled.

The oldster stumbled, and one foot stepped over the dead-line, then another.

Rifles crashed.

Hit hard, the old man dropped to the ground, groaned from somewhere deep inside him, then lay still and silent.

The cabin door closed.

"Yee-haw!" Thornton yelled, pumping a fist into the air.

Around him men laughed.

But others didn't.

Drake saw eight or nine men standing around the fires, backs stiff, their faces like stone.

The senseless slaughter of a defenseless old man had not sat well with the more professional gunfighters and they were letting their feelings show.

It dawned on Drake then that Thornton, and the Fat Man, had made their first mistake.

A mistake that could return to haunt them.

Chapter 23

"He was somebody's grandfather," Withers said. "But I imagine they can't feel the hurt anymore."

Sickened by what he'd seen, Drake looked up at the Pinkerton, who was standing at the entrance to the tent.

"More dead farmers, huh?"

"Sounds like," Withers said.

"Why are we here?" Drake said.

"Insurance. You heard the man."

"What kind of insurance?"

"If the Fat Man's terror tactics don't work and people don't flee the valley, he'll come up with another plan."

"And where do we come in?"

"Why, we're the mad-dog killers who committed all the murders. Thornton shoots us and turns our bodies over to Marshal Halloran."

Withers took a seat on his cot.

"'Caught these boys red-handed, Marshal,' Thornton says. 'They tried to kill and rob a couple of members of my hunting party.' 'You did good,' Halloran says. 'But I would have liked to have hung them my own self.' 'They put up a fight,' Thornton says. 'I didn't have a choice.' 'Well,' Halloran says, 'their killing days are done, an' that's what counts, huh?'"

Withers smiled. "That's how it will be. All tied up neat with ribbons and bows."

Drake shook his head. "It's too thin. The Fat Man will never get away with it."

"He can, Mr. Drake. And he will."

"That sounds like a death sentence."

"It is, Mr. Drake."

Drake was silent for a few moments, then said, "We have to escape from here."

"Indeed we do. But how?"

"I'll study on it."

"Not for too long, I hope. Stuffy in here." Withers opened the tent flap. "Hah, here's something." He turned. "Take a look, Mr. Drake."

Drake rose and looked outside. He was in time to see Helen Lee stop at the dead-line. One of the guards waved her forward and she stepped into the cabin.

"Miss Lee is trying to sell her peace talk," Drake said. "Do you think she'll succeed?"

"Depends what she has to offer."

"A lot."

"Unless the Fat Man is more interested in assets than ass."

"Yeah, there's always that."

"Chauncey Drake!"

Thornton stopped outside the tent.

"Get out here. You and What's-His-Name."

Drake stepped outside, his intense hatred for Thornton obvious in his unrestrained glare. "What the hell do you want?"

"The Fat Man needs to see both of you."

"Why?"

"How the hell should I know? Get your asses over there to the dead-line and wait until you're ordered forward."

"What do you think he wants?" Drake said.

"To offer us tea and crumpets maybe," Withers said.

"I doubt it."

"Me too."

"Then why?"

"Mr. Drake, do I have a sign around my neck that says 'Oracle'?"

"What's an oracle?"

"Someone who can see into the future."

"You're not one of them."

"No, I'm not."

"You two, no talking on the line," a guard yelled. He was a tall man with a scrawny neck and a carrion eater's eyes.

After a couple of minutes, he said, "Step forward slowly, hands out by your sides where I can see them."

Drake and Withers did as they were told. The guards searched them thoroughly, then said, "Walk to the door, and stop."

The second guard, short and stocky, carrying a Henry rifle, said, "Did Thornton tell you to put a pinch of dung in your noses?"

"No," Drake said. "And if he had, I wouldn't have done it."

The man smiled. "Your funeral. When you go inside, you're gonna wish you was sniffing horseshit."

A few moments later someone tapped three times on the inside of the cabin door. The stocky man opened it.

"Enter, gentlemen," he said. He was grinning.

Drake and Withers plunged into darkness as the door closed behind them.

Then the stench hit with the force of a sledgehammer.

The foulness was a living entity, as though the air was filled with curling maggots. It stuck in the throat and assailed the nostrils, triggering a gag reflex in Drake so severe that his mouth filled with saliva and dry heaves thrust upward in his belly as though they were being driven by a fist.

Beside him, Withers looked like a man in distress. Drake heard the Pinkerton's breath wheeze in his chest and the *gulp*, *gulp*, sound of a man swallowing down his urge to puke.

Then, from somewhere in the darkness, "Please, gentlemen, come forward a little so I can see you clearer. I so very rarely have guests."

Chapter 24

Battling the desire to be violently sick, Chauncey Drake breathed through his mouth as his eyes became accustomed to the gloom.

What he saw appalled him.

The creature on the oversized cot was naked, a monstrosity of sweating, stinking flesh that almost swamped its bed, like a vast mound of rising white bread dough overflowing a bowl.

The eyes were lost, pushed almost shut by the fat cheeks, the nose like a pig snout, the mouth small and pink and cruel.

He could have been ten years old, or a hundred.

But the voice that emanated from the grotesque body was almost cultured, as smooth as velvet polishing glass.

"Miss Helen Lee, I think you have met," the Fat Man said. "This other person is a slave and her name does not matter." His mouth moved in what could have been a smile. "I can't pronounce it anyway."

A small, slender Chinese girl, who looked to be no

more than fourteen years old, stood beside the top of the bed.

Drake's gaze turned to the girl. She showed no interest in anything around her, staring straight ahead, her eyes empty. She was dead, still breathing, her heart beating, but dead.

"Ah, yes, Mr. Drake," the Fat Man said with striking perception, "she's not much for conversation, but she has her uses."

Helen Lee made a small sound that could have been a repressed retch.

The Fat Man chose not to ignore it. His mouth grimaced again.

"Miss Lee caught us, shall we say, in *fragrate delicti*. For some reason it disturbed her."

"Not at all," Helen Lee said.

"You're a liar," the Fat Man said.

A silence, then he said, "Do you know why you and your friend are here, Mr. Drake?" He raised a pudgy hand. "By the way, thank you for accepting my invitation. You young people are all so busy nowadays, dashing this way and that. I declare, sometimes you make me quite dizzy." His head moved on the pillow. "Now, where was I? Oh, yes, do you know why I invited you?"

Drake looked at Withers, but the Pinkerton was battling his weak stomach, alone in his misery, and made no attempt to answer.

"No, we don't," Drake said finally.

"Miss Lee wants me to end my, ah, campaign against the squatters in this valley. She said we need persuasion, not bullets, to get them off the land."

The Fat Man reached out a flabby, enormous arm

and slammed the palm of his hand hard against the Chinese girl's face.

"Get away from me, you sniveling bitch," he said. "Over there in the corner, where you belong."

The girl, her head bowed, shuffled away like a silent ghost.

Then, as though nothing had happened, the Fat Man continued, "I must admit, so far all my endeavors have not borne fruit. The squatters are still here, occupying lands worth millions."

He raised a hand again. "Do you see my dilemma, Mr. Drake?"

"I see it."

"Your opinion, please. Believe me. I will value it most highly. That's why I asked you here."

"The settlers won't run," Drake said. "Farmers, ranchers, townspeople, they'll fight you."

The Fat Man clapped his hands, a weak gesture that sounded like the flap of butterfly wings.

"You have stated the case most clearly, Mr. Drake. Yes, very succinct and to the point. Indeed, they will fight."

He turned and looked at Helen Lee. "Your point also, my dear."

"I know I can persuade them to sell," the woman said.

"Yes, perhaps. But what's in it for me?"

"One million dollars. A finder's fee."

"Little enough for all my hard work."

The Fat Man lay back on his pillow.

After a few moments, he said, "What I propose is this: a demonstration in force, say, three nights hence. One night of terror during which we kill dozens, perhaps hundreds."

His eyes sought out Drake. "Green Meadow is the center, the hub of this resistance. Destroy the town and every man, woman, and child in it, and all resistance could collapse.

"If it fails, then we'll do the business Miss Lee's way."

"You can't destroy a town." This from Withers, talking through clenched teeth, either trying to hold down his anger or his gorge.

"Oh, but I can," the Fat Man said, "and I will. You see, I've done it before."

Chapter 25

"Ah, does that surprise you, gentlemen?" the Fat Man said. "The light is dim in here, but I can see it does."

Drake felt a sudden fatigue, worn out by the stench of the Fat Man's body and the rancidity of his conversation. The creature was talking again.

"During the late War of Northern Aggression, I had the honor to serve under the great Southern patriot and guerilla leader, Captain William Clarke Quantrill. I joined him in the fall of 1862, and then, on August 21, 1863, came a day of glory that will echo through the ages. Remember that date well, gentlemen."

"I already know the date," Withers said, surprising Drake. "That's the day Quantrill raided Lawrence, Kansas, massacred two hundred unarmed men and half-grown boys, then torched the town. A low, cowardly act if ever there was one."

"Well, Withers," Drake whispered, "that ripped it."

The Fat Man quivered and raised his head off the pillow. His voice was no longer quiet.

"Liar!" he screamed. "Damned liar! The town was a

traitorous rat's nest of abolitionists, Redlegs, and Jay-hawkers. It was a military action, damn your eyes, not a massacre."

The Fat Man turned his head. "Bell! Bell! Bell!"

The Chinese girl began yanking on a rope hanging in the corner. Immediately a bell on the roof clamored, its brassy clang earsplitting in the room.

The door crashed open and the two guards charged inside.

"Him! The traitor!" the Fat Man screamed, pointing at Withers. "Take him away. I'll decide the manner of his death later."

The guards grabbed the Pinkerton and dragged him outside. The door slammed shut again as the bell chimed to a halt.

"I'll hang that snake in the grass," the Fat Man said, "from the highest tree I can find."

Drake tried a desperation play, knowing that he was trying to buck a stacked deck with a busted flush.

"He's a Yankee," he said. "He doesn't know any better."

"A Yankee? From where?"

Drake hesitated, then said, "Philadelphia."

"Damn his soul to hell, the worst kind of Yankee."

"He doesn't know how the South suffered," Drake said, knowing he was crawling like a worm.

"Indeed he does not. He proved that with his words."

Drake pushed it. "You can't hang a man for ignorance." He hoped his smile was sincere. "Even a Yankee."

The Fat Man was silent.

Fear spiked at Drake's stomach. He'd pushed too hard. Way too hard.

"I will make that decision later," the Fat Man said finally.

It was not even a glimmer of hope, but Drake clutched at it.

"Thank you," he said.

The Fat Man ignored him.

"Miss Lee, stand beside Mr. Drake. I have something to say to you both."

Helen Lee did as she was told.

"Your friend was right, Mr. Drake. We did kill two hundred Yankees in Lawrence, six of them by my own hand. I took their scalps and hung them on my horse's bridle. After we left, it took that damned town months to recover."

The Fat Man waved a hand, an effort that left him wheezing.

"Green Meadow will not recover."

"I beg you to let me convince the town to sell out to us," Helen Lee said. There was a note of desperation in her voice.

"No," the Fat Man said. "I won't tell you this again, dear lady. My way first, then yours. Don't back talk me again."

Drake pushed it again, amazed at his own stupidity.

"You can't take the town with twenty men," he said.

"You are quite correct, Mr. Drake, but I will have more men here in a few days. Thirty hired gunmen arrived in the settlement of Wilburton yesterday by rail, all of them Texans. Mr. Thornton assures me that when it comes to slaughter, they are the best of the best."

The Fat Man made a grimace that passed for a smile.

"Once my reinforcements arrive, I will destroy Green

Meadow with fifty men. When I'm finished, not even grass will grow in that accursed place or the birds sing."

His head flopped back on the pillow.

"Now leave me. I grow weary."

"About Withers . . ."

"I will decide his punishment later. Get out of here, both of you."

Drake, a sense of defeat weighing on him, opened the door and stepped outside. He breathed deeply, getting the vile stink out of his lungs.

The guards laughed, then pushed him back across the dead-line.

Chapter 26

"He plans to hang you. Count on it," Drake said.

"I know. That's why there's a guard outside the tent," Withers said.

"Do you always make friends wherever you go?"

"The man's a monster, Mr. Drake. A born killer."

"I know, but did you really have to tell him?"

"Yes, I believe I did."

"Thank you for that." Drake shook his head. "Now we have no choice. We'll have to put a whole passel of gone between the Fat Man and us."

"Easier said than done, Mr. Drake."

Drake's voice dropped to a whisper. "We're getting out of here tonight."

"With a guard at the tent and Thornton's gunmen all around us?"

"Come dark, we'll make our break."

"Sounds like a grandstand play that's destined to end badly."

"Withers, study on it. Do you have a better idea?"

"No studying needed. Anything is better than hanging."

"Then we'll sit tight in the meantime. At full dark, we light a shuck."

"What about the guard?"

"I'll take care of him."

"How?"

"I don't know."

"Then I'm as good as dead already."

"Go right ahead, Withers. Throw up the sponge before we even get started."

"Sorry, Mr. Drake. I guess the Fat Man depressed me more than I realized."

"Imagine how depressed the folks in Green Meadow will feel if we don't warn them in time."

"It will be another Lawrence, Kansas."

"Yeah, only this time the Fat Man is in command and he'll kill everybody in town."

As the day shaded into evening the sky turned pale lilac, streaked with ribbons of scarlet and jade. But purple thunderheads were building over the great arc of the Sans Bois Mountains to the west and the tent canvas flapped in a rising wind.

Drake studied the threatening weather with some satisfaction.

"If it rains, there will be no moon," he said. "The darker it is, the better our chances."

"Where is Rockefeller?"

"Huh?" Drake said, surprised by a question out of the blue.

"He'll have no truck with the Fat Man's plans."

Drake turned from the tent flap and looked at Withers. "I reckon he's back in New York or Boston or wherever it is millionaires hang their hats," he said.

"Not if Miss Lee is working for him."

"You think he could still be around somewhere?"

"It's possible, waiting to see how things pan out."

Drake considered that, then said, "Here or there, it makes no difference to us."

"Why did Rockefeller try to shortchange the settlers?"

"Because that's what rich men do—buy cheap and sell dear."

"If there are millions involved, he could have upped the ante, spent some pocket change. Why didn't he?"

Drake was silent for a long time; then he said, "Withers, what are you driving at?"

"I don't know. Just thinking aloud."

"Then don't. Better still, think about how we're going to get away from here." He shook his head. "Wherever he is, John D. Rockefeller ain't thinking about you. Or me."

An hour later, the rain started with a rhythmic *tick, tick, tick* on the tent roof and thunder boomed in the distance.

The storm grew in intensity and lightning flashed above the clearing, briefly silhouetting the tall figure of the guard outside the tent.

The man stepped closer.

"You in the tent."

"What do you want?" Drake said. "There's no room in here."

The guard ignored that and said, "The ranny with the beard gets hung tomorrow at dawn."

"How do you know?" Drake said, instantly realizing what a stupid question that was.

"Word just came down. The charge is high treason against the Confederate States of America."

A hand appeared through the flap, fisted around the handle of a bowie knife.

"Cut your way out of the tent," the guard said. "I'll be looking someplace else."

Drake opened the flap enough to see the guard's face. He was one of the disapproving gunmen he'd seen standing around the fires when the old blind man was murdered.

"What's your name?" Drake asked. "I'll remember it."

"The name is Chris. Now beat it."

"Chris, if we escape, the Fat Man will kill you for sure."

"I don't intend to stick around. Killing old men and women and children don't sit right with me."

"Chris, thanks."

Whatever the gunman said was lost in a blast of thunder.

Drake stepped to the back of the tent and plunged the keen blade of the bowie knife into the canvas.

Chapter 27

Drake and Withers crouched at the back of the tent, lashed by a torrential rain. Twenty-five yards of open country separated them from a rim of hardwoods. Beyond the hickories, a high peak rose gradually, heavily forested with oak and pine.

His heart hammering in his ears, Drake studied the distances.

Despite the constant lightning flashes, the chances of them being seen in the downpour were small.

This wasn't a soldiers' camp where pickets were posted no matter the weather. Apart from their own guard, and the two at the door to the cabin, the gunmen had sought their tents and the clearing was deserted.

"Make for the trees," Drake whispered. "Then keep on going."

Withers nodded. The Pinkerton seemed nervous, as though he expected a shouted challenge or a gunshot at any moment.

"Go!" Drake said.

He sprinted for the hardwoods, Withers pounding beside him.

They reached the hickory rim without incident, then plunged into the thicker pines and oaks. The land tilted upward, muddy and made treacherous underfoot by darkness and loose shale.

Withers tripped on a root, fell on his side, then tumbled back down the slope. Drake waited for him to make the climb again, his chest heaving.

"You hurt?" he asked when the Pinkerton joined him.

Withers shook his head. "Lost my footing."

"Figured that," Drake said. "Let's go."

Lightning flickered among the trees, brief, searing moments of white that made the following darkness even more impenetrable. The rain hissed like an angry dragon, soaking and relentless.

After thirty minutes of climbing, Drake calculated they were about six or seven hundred feet above the flat, heading into a high country of craggy, sandstone ridges and stunted cedar.

They were stopped by a rock wall, the sandstone undercut to a depth of about three feet. There was room for two crouching men to shelter under the overhang and Drake grabbed Withers by the arm and dragged him into its meager shelter.

"Rest," he said, sitting on wet shale. "I'm all used up."

Withers made no protest and Drake heard him groan as he dropped onto his butt.

"Fifteen minutes, then we have to move on," Drake said.

"To where?"

"I don't know. Anyplace but here."

To his joy, Drake's makings were still dry, protected by his coat, and he built a cigarette.

"You think they'll come after us?" Withers asked.

"Bet on it. We're the Fat Man's insurance policy, remember."

"After he raids Green Meadow, that no longer holds. He can't blame the massacre of a couple of hundred people on a pair of mad-dog killers."

Drake thumbed a match into flame and lit his smoke.

"He can't get away with it, Withers, even in the Indian Territory. When an entire town is wiped out, the federal authorities tend to take notice."

Lightning flared, making a skull of the Pinkerton's face.

"A quick in—destroy the town," he said. "Then a quick out—head for Texas. If anyone questions him, his lawyers will say he was never even in Oklahoma."

Withers turned his head, trying to make out Drake in the darkness.

"Lawrence came back after Quantrill's raid a bigger and busier city than before. But Green Meadow is only a two-bit cow town and it won't. Nobody will want to rebuild there, and pretty soon it will be just another burned-out ghost in the middle of nowhere."

The Pinkerton reached out and took the cigarette from between Drake's fingers. He placed it between his lips.

"Build yourself another, Mr. Drake. I don't know how."

"What about the farms and the ranches?" Drake said, busy with tobacco and papers.

"When the town dies, they will die. The town sustains them. Without Green Meadow there are only miles of empty prairie."

"And the land? The oil? The millions to be made?"

"Rockefeller moves in and drills his wells. Him or somebody else."

Drake looked into the darkness and rain. "You paint a bleak picture, Withers."

"Not so bleak. You and I stand in the way of everybody's plans."

"So we got it to do."

"That's how it shapes up."

Drake's cigarette butt spiraled, sparking, into the night.

"Then let's head for Green Meadow."

"You may have to go most of the way alone, Mr. Drake. My bullet wound has weakened me."

"We both go, or we don't go at all. And for God's sake, quit calling me Mr. Drake."

"How about Chauncey?"

"It'll do," Drake said, rising to his feet.

It was still dark when he and Withers passed the high-shouldered bulk of Little Yancy Mountain and onto the flat a mile north of Rock Creek.

As the night shaded into a sodden dawn, the cottonwoods along the creek came in sight.

And that's where Harvey Thornton and seven of his riders found them.

Chapter 28

Harvey Thornton was judge, jury, and executioner, and there was no appeal to his higher values because he had none.

He was a man without conscience or compassion, but was loyal to his own hard code, the law of the frontier that demanded a man keep his word.

Thornton had promised Drake that if he tried to escape he would lose the fingers of his left hand.

He kept that promise.

First Drake.

Then Withers.

But, to make a sport of the thing, he stripped them naked and ran them for a while.

When Drake or Withers stumbled and fell, Thornton and his riders laid into them with rope ends, stiff, wet lashes that cut to the bone.

After a while Thornton grew bored with the sport. The men's fingers were splayed on the fallen trunk of a cottonwood and shot away.

"I gave you fair warning," Thornton said. "Now you have suffered the consequences."

Drake and Withers huddled beside the log, cradling stumps that hurt and bled.

The gunman did not take them back to camp. As a good joke, he took their clothes and left them naked, saying only, "Later we'll look for you and bury you, if the wolves and coyotes don't beat us to it."

Thornton and his men rode away, laughing, slapping each other on the back.

And still the rain came down.

Chauncey Drake had never felt hatred before. He felt it now.

It was a black, brooding cancer in the gut, a devouring emotion that can unhinge a man and make him worse than he ever was before.

It was a desire to kill.

And with it, the will to live long enough to exact revenge, a bastard child of hatred.

"We have to move, Withers," Drake said, staggering to his feet. "Find shelter for a spell."

The Pinkerton looked up at Drake. "Leave me be, Chauncey. Let me die right here."

"Get up, damn you," Drake said. "I'm not letting you quit on me."

"I'm a dead man already."

"You're not dead. And we still have a job to do."

Withers raised the stump of his left hand, blood running down his hairy forearm. "Look at that! Tell me I'm not a dead man!"

"Are you an example of what the Pinkertons are hiring these days, Withers?"

"Go to hell."

"You're a damned poor excuse for a Pinkerton and an even poorer excuse for a man."

"Chauncey Drake, you bastard, give it up. You're dead. Like me, dead, dead, dead."

"I don't plan on dying, Withers. Not until I kill Thornton and the Fat Man, I don't. Hate is going to keep me alive, and you."

Drake took Withers by the elbow of his good arm. "Get on your goddamned feet."

"And go where?"

"We need shelter and rest. If we don't move around too much it will help the bleeding stop."

"I can't, Chauncey. I can't make it anywhere."

"You can make it. I'll help you. Now, on your feet."

Withers got to his feet, a small, bearded man who appeared to be shrinking in the rain.

His arm around the Pinkerton's shoulders, Drake helped him away from the creek and half carried him toward the nearest stand of trees.

The downpour closed around them like a gusting gray curtain as they staggered forward and disappeared into a band of hickory and oak.

The land did nothing to mark their passing and the rain and the trees whispered to one another as before, indifferent to the petty troubles of naked men.

Chapter 29

It was shelter of a sort, a narrow cut in the forest floor roofed by a couple of fallen hickories. Ferns grew in abundance around the spot and Drake used these to make a nest under the trees.

The shelter was fairly dry, out of the wind, and Drake and Withers lay close, sharing body heat.

But Withers was not doing well. He was older than Drake, and the wounds he'd suffered took a greater toll on him. He shivered uncontrollably and his face was ashen.

Drake closed his eyes, thinking of hot coffee, sweetened with a shot of Hennessey. Right now it would be a lifesaver. But he had none of that. Only pain and the hatred that crawled, rank in his belly.

He looked at the stumps of his fingers. They had stopped bleeding, but the wounds were raw and red, white bone showing.

But it was not his gun hand.

He was thankful for that.

Now all he wanted was a blue Colt and six feet of ground between him and Thornton.

He was not a praying man, but he did now, begging for life, another day or two or three, enough time to settle with Harvey Thornton.

Then he realized he was asking God to help him kill a man. He was sure that had not set well with the Almighty, and the lightning that struck close by made him certain of it.

"Chauncey," Withers said, his voice weak and uncertain, "I'm damned cold."

Drake covered the little man with ferns. "Help any?"

"Not much."

A pause, then, "When do we move out, Chauncey?"

"A couple more hours."

"I can't do that."

"Damn right you can do that. I'll carry you on my shoulders if I have to."

"Leave me. You're already exhausted and I'll just slow you up."

"Nobody's leaving nobody. When I go, you go."

"Chauncey . . ."

"What?"

"Nothing. Nothing at all."

Despite the fire in his stump, the cold and ticking rain, and his concern for Withers, Drake closed his eyes and dozed.

When he woke, he didn't know if he'd been asleep for minutes or hours.

He turned his head to look at Withers.

The little man was gone.

Drake got to his feet, swayed, and his raw stump hit the trunk of one of the fallen trees. A shock of white-hot pain made him cry out. Then he dropped to his knees, head bent, whimpering his misery.

He looked up through the tree canopy at the leaden sky, the hopelessness of his situation weighing heavy on him. It would be so easy to crawl back under the trees and sleep and never wake up.

So easy . . . without pain . . . just . . . oblivion . . .

Then he remembered Thornton, the grin on his face, his glaring tattooed eye, as he shot his fingers off one by one. There would be no sleep. Only the harsh reality of this waking nightmare.

Drake struggled to his feet.

"Withers!"

The trees whispered and rustled in surprise, but there was no other sound.

"Damn you, Withers! I'm gonna whup your ass! Where the hell are you?"

Drake felt as though he was shouting into a gale, his words falling around him unheard, like dead leaves.

He searched among the trees until his throat was hoarse from shouting and his feet were bruised and lacerated from thorns and hidden rocks.

After an hour he gave up.

Withers was gone and a man who didn't want to be found could lose himself forever in the deep woods.

A sadness in him, Drake appreciated the little Pinkerton's sacrifice. In the end, he'd proven himself a man of integrity and courage.

Drake would always remember that, and perhaps one day he would use it as Reuben Withers's epitaph.

Drake walked from the trees, then directed his steps eastward, toward Green Meadow.

He had it to do.

Chapter 30

Drake walked for the rest of the day, and that night fell in with thieves.

Staggering from hunger, pain, and exhaustion, he saw the flicker of a campfire among the trees.

Wary, he stopped in the darkness. Was it some of Thornton's men?

Limping on sore feet, Drake slowly made his way closer. The rain had stopped a couple of hours earlier, but heat lightning flashed to the north and the wind was still a force to be reckoned with.

Invisible in the gloom, he got as near as he dared and got down on one knee, his eyes scanning the men around the fire.

There were four of them, three standing and another lying in his blankets. A ways back from the circle of firelight, horses were picketed along with a pack mule.

None of the men looked familiar, and one in a white hat and vest looked like he could be an Indian.

Drake doubted that he could last through another night without heat and food, and he decided to take a chance. All he had to lose was his life, at that moment, not a very valuable commodity.

He stepped closer. "Hello, the camp!"

Instantly the three men were alert, their guns at the ready. The fourth man did not leave his blankets.

"Who's out there? Identify yourself."

"Name's Chauncey Drake."

"Are you on the scout?"

"You could say that."

"Come on in real slow and we don't want to see your hands anywhere near a gun."

"Mister," Drake said, "the only gun I got is the one between my legs."

Drake stepped forward, through the trees, then into the circle of the firelight.

The oldest of the three, a lanky man with iron gray hair and a huge dragoon mustache, took one look at Drake and said, "What the hell are you?"

"A gambler who fell on hard times."

"Ace, I can see you ain't prospering," the lanky man said. "How come you're nekkid as a scalded hog?"

"I was robbed," Drake said. He showed the stump of his hand. "Got my fingers shot off."

Drake was correct in identifying one of the men as an Indian. He was short, stocky, his black hair hanging in two thick braids twined with red ribbon.

He quickly stepped to Drake, took his arm, and examined his mutilated hand.

"How is it, Patch?"

"Bad," the man called Patch said. "He's bled out some. I don't see no rot, though."

"Get him over here to the fire and find a blanket for him. Man looks like he's dead on his feet."

"I got to do something with that hand, Luke," Patch said.

"Hell, leave him be, Injun. He's nothing to us."

This from the third man, who'd been standing by the fire. He was tall, skinny as a whip, with a small, tight mouth as though he was sucking on a lemon.

"He's on the scout, Andy," Luke said, "just like us. That makes him almost kin."

"We've been lucky so far, Luke," Andy said. "This man carries bad luck with him. I can see it in him plain."

"Hell, he's been robbed, stripped, and his fingers shot off," Luke said. "I'd say you can see his bad luck plain, all right. But it don't mean he carries it around."

"Try telling Joe Flores we've been lucky so far," Patch said.

"I don't take back talk or sass from an Injun," Andy said, his eyes ugly.

Patch laid a blanket over Drake's shoulders, then slowly straightened. He wore a Colt high on his right hip and he was ready.

"Well, I sassed you, Andy. What you going to do about it?"

"Enough!" Luke said. "Any draw and shoot to be done, I'll do it."

He pointed to the man covered with a blanket.

"Ol' Joe ain't been dead for an hour yet and we're already squabbling among ourselves."

"What does he care?" Andy said. "He's already stoking furnaces in hell."

"Yeah, but he's looking down on us, or up at us, or wherever the hell he's looking, and thinking to himself we're a sorry bunch."

Luke took a step back.

"Patch, you want to skin that revolver, try it on me. Same goes for you, Andy."

"Ah, the hell with it," Andy said. He dropped beside the fire and stared into the flames.

"Patch," Luke said, "go about your business."

"Anything you say, Luke," the Indian said.

He found Drake a cup and poured him coffee.

"I'll bind up that hand," he said. "It's all I can do for you."

"It's enough, and I appreciate it," Drake said.

Luke sat by the fire and took a frying pan off the flames. He looked at Drake. "What did you say your name was again?"

"Chauncey Drake."

"Well, Chauncey, we got an antelope steak left. You want to make a trial of it?"

Drake was enjoying the hot coffee and his hunger had left him.

"Maybe later."

"Just say."

"I could use a smoke, though, real bad."

Luke passed over his makings and Drake built a cigarette.

"You know who robbed you?" Andy said. "Maybe it was folks we know."

It was not a friendly question, but Drake answered it.

"Yeah"—he inhaled smoke deeply—"man called Harvey Thornton." He hesitated briefly, then said, "He killed my partner."

Andy whistled between his teeth.

"Harvey Thornton! You're lucky you still got your hair."

"I aim to lift his scalp," Drake said.

"You gonna call him out, like?"

"Whatever it takes."

"You agin Harvey Thornton." Andy snorted. "That'll be a sight to see."

Even Patch, binding up Drake's hand, grinned at that.

Drake ignored Andy and the grins. "I could sure use some more coffee," he said.

Luke refilled his cup. "You say you're on the scout, Chauncey. From what law?"

"Marshal of a town west of here."

"What did you do?"

"They say I murdered a whore. I didn't."

"Nah"—Andy grinned—"a brave, gunfighting man like you who's gonna lift Harvey Thornton's scalp don't kill whores."

"Back off," Drake said, his temper flaring.

"Are you gonna make me?"

"Andy!" Luke snapped. "Let it go."

"He sassed me."

"Let it go. The man's half dead, for God's sake."

Luke looked at Drake. "We robbed a bank north of here, up in the Brushy Mountain country. That was a week ago and we've been on the scout since."

"Where you headed?" Drake said.

"Back to Texas. Figured we'd take Joe with us. If he don't stink too bad."

Luke glanced at the dead man. "Joe Flores was hell on wheels with a Colt's gun, killed eight men in his day. Damn kid shot him with a squirrel rifle as he was leaving the bank. He lingered for a spell, but then died."

"Too bad," Drake said.

"Is that all you got to say?" Andy said.

"What more is there to say?"

"Well, you could be more respect—"

Andy never finished his sentence. His head exploded . . . adding an exclamation point at the end of his life.

Chapter 31

A big man riding a tall bay horse rode out of the trees, the butt of a Sharps .50 on his thigh.

"Don't try it, Luke. You neither, Indian. You know me. I'll kill you."

Luke, his face spattered with Andy's blood and brains, had no fight in him. Patch was tense, thinking it over.

The rider read the signs.

The Sharps slapped into the palm of this left hand, leveled at the Indian's belly.

"Patch, you got two options. Unbuckle your gun belt or die right where you stand."

"Damn you, Washita, damn you to hell," Patch said.

"Make your choice or make your play."

The Indian hesitated; then his hands went to the buckle of his gun belt.

"Left hand, Patch. You're slick, and I won't take any chances with you."

The holster and cartridge belt thudded at the Indian's feet.

The man called Washita turned to Luke.

"That Joe Flores under the blanket?"

Luke nodded. "Kid shot him with a—"

"I know what the kid did," Washita said. Then, conversationally, "Drop your guns, Luke."

The older man did as he was told without protest.

Drake rose to his feet. He pointed at Andy. "You murdered that man."

The gray eyes Washita turned on him were the coldest Drake had ever seen, the hard eyes of a born killer.

"Who the hell are you?" the man said.

"A wayfarer," Drake said.

"Well, sit back on your ass, Wayfarer."

The muzzle of the Sharps moved an inch. That was all it took.

Drake sat down again.

"It ain't none of your business, Wayfarer, but I'll tell you anyhow," Washita said. "Andy Ronson was fast with a gun and mean as a rattler, and I reckoned he was liable to make a play. I'm not a man who takes chances, as you probably figured by now, so I took him out of the fight first."

The rider pulled back his slicker, showing the deputy marshal's star on his shirt. "Name's Washita Jolly out of Judge Isaac Parker's court."

The cold eyes pinned Drake to the darkness behind him.

"What name do you go by, Wayfarer?"

"Chauncey Drake, the one I was born with."

Washita Jolly turned to Luke. "Was he with you on the bank job?"

"Never seen him before until a hour ago," Luke said.

"Came in naked as a scalded hog with the fingers of his left hand shot off. Claimed he was robbed by Harvey Thornton. Says Thornton killed his partner."

Jolly's gray eyes didn't merely observe a man. They attacked him.

"Is what Luke says true? You were robbed by Harvey Thornton?"

"Yes, it's true, and I mean to kill him first chance I get."

"Good luck on that one. Show me your hand."

Drake held up the bandaged stump.

Jolly grunted, thinking things over. But his stare was everywhere, especially on Patch. The Indian was surly, his black eyes reckless, as though he might go for it.

Finally the lawman said, "Don't seem like Thornton. Murder, rape, now that I could believe. But robbing pilgrims was never his style."

"It was earlier today," Drake said. "And he has no style."

Jolly stepped out of the saddle, his eyes on Patch. He stepped to the edge of the firelight, his mouth drawn tight under his mustache.

"Indian," he said, "you're making me downright uneasy. Maybe it's because you're a thinking man. I don't like men who think too deep, especially Apaches."

He looked at Drake. "You, Wayfarer, there are shackles in my saddlebags. Bring them."

"I only got one hand."

"Yeah, I know. Make two trips."

Drake rose to his feet, but Patch's voice stopped him.

"Washita, you're not chaining me like a dog," he said.

Jolly smiled. "My, my, Patch, your life is boiling down

to a series of little choices, ain't it? Now you got to pick between wearing the irons or getting a bullet in the belly."

He leveled the Sharps. "I'm not a patient man, so speak up. What's it to be?"

The Indian's defiance melted. He stared at the ground and Jolly said, "I thought so." He waved Drake forward. "Get the shackles, Wayfarer."

Drake found the chains in the saddlebags and hefted them in his hand. He thought briefly about hitting Jolly over the head with them. But dismissed the idea as an excellent way to commit suicide.

The lawman had Luke shackle Patch's hands behind his back; then the Indian did the same to the older man.

"Well-done, boys," Jolly said. "Now we can all sit and enjoy a cup of coffee and some good conversation."

"What are you going to do with me?" Drake asked.

Jolly thought about that, then shrugged. "Nothing, I guess."

Drake watched the man empty dregs from a cup, then refill it with coffee.

"You on the scout?" Jolly asked, settling the pot back on the fire.

Drake made no answer, and the deputy said, "It don't matter none. I don't have a warrant on you." He looked Drake over, and seemed less than impressed. "Just as well, you'd be more trouble than you're worth."

Drake was not impressed with Jolly either, but he was the only lawman around.

Knowing he could be making a big mistake, he took a breath and plunged ahead. "Deputy, I need your help."

Jolly smiled. "A lot of folks need my help. What's your problem?"

"It will take some time in the telling."

"No matter. We got all night."

Drake cradled his throbbing hand in the crook of his right arm, then told his story, beginning with the murder of Loretta Sinclair, ending with the Fat Man's planned attack on Green Meadow.

Washita Jolly had listened in silence; now he turned to Luke. "What do you think?" he asked. "About the story, I mean."

The outlaw's shackles clanked as he sought a softer piece of ground for his butt. "He got his fingers shot off. A man don't think straight after that."

Jolly nodded. "Patch, what are you thinking?"

"That I'd like to sink my knife into your belly."

"Ah, so you have no opinion on the matter one way or t'other."

Jolly looked at Drake. "John D. Rockefeller, you say?"

"Yeah, and his friend Karl Benz."

"Right, and Karl is a German, from Germany."

"Yes."

"And they was here?"

"I told you, this country is swimming in oil and they want it."

"What fer?"

"For the fuel to power horseless carriages."

"And this ranny, the Fat Man, he also wants the oil?"

"No, just the money he can get from Rockefeller after he drives the settlers off the land."

"Ah, now I see. And does the Fat Man want a horseless carriage?"

"I don't know."

"And this woman, Helen Lee—"

"That's not her real name."

"No? Then what's her real name?"

"I can't remember."

"But, anyhow, she wants the land."

"Yes."

Jolly smiled. "Son, oil ain't worth spit."

"But it will be, when every family in the country has a horseless carriage."

"What are we going to do with all the horses?"

"Huh?"

"If everybody has a horseless carriage, it's going to put a lot of horses out of business. What will we do with them all?"

"I don't know."

"Sell them to John D. Rockefeller, maybe?"

Drake was silent for a few moments; then he said, "You don't believe me, do you?"

"It's a wild story, Wayfarer . . . financiers, horseless carriages—which ain't never gonna happen, by the way—dead whores, fat men, beautiful women, massacres . . . a lot for a man to swallow"—he made a face—"like this damned coffee."

"Every word I told you is true."

"And in your own mind, I'm sure it is. But you're a mite teched in the head, boy, what with losing your fingers and getting robbed an' all. Best you sleep for a spell."

Drake choked down his disappointment like a rock. He could count on no help from Jolly.

Or anybody.

Chapter 32

Drake slept by the fire, wrapped in his blanket. The pain in his hand woke him twice. He woke a third time when Jolly tossed wood on the fire.

He woke with the dawn. Jolly already had the horses saddled and he'd freed Luke's hands long enough for him to make coffee.

Jolly saw Drake sit up and squatted in front of him.

"How you feeling, Wayfarer?"

"Still teched."

The deputy missed the irony. "When a man's brains are scrambled, it takes time to put them back together again." He smiled. "I've been thinking about you."

"Thinking what?"

"That I'm not going to throw you all naked into the world. Not Washita Jolly's style, you understand." He nodded over his shoulder. "I found a shirt and pants in Luke's pack, socks too, but they got holes in them. Take Joe's boots. He's got no more use for them."

"Marshal, I need a gun and a horse," Drake said.

By the fire, Luke nodded. "A gun for sure." He gave

Jolly a sidelong glance. "Man never knows when he's gonna run into a snake."

"Boy, I'm doing a lot for you, giving you stuff I usually confiscate," Jolly said. "I hope you remember it."

He took out a tally book and a stub of pencil.

"You can take Joe Flores's gray mustang, his saddle, and tack. He's got a Winchester rifle, a Colt, and a holster and cartridge belt."

Jolly chewed on the end of his pencil.

"Let's call it twenty for the horse, forty for saddle and tack, eighteen dollars for the rifle, and a dollar-fifty extry on account of the octagon barrel. I'll throw in the rifle scabbard and gun belt gratis."

The marshal did some quick calculations in his book, then said, "Young man, you owe me seventy-nine dollars and fifty cents."

Drake opened his blanket, revealing his nakedness. "Look at me. Do I have a place to carry a wallet?"

"Figured that," Jolly said. "As soon as you can, you'll mail the money to me. Address it to Deputy Marshal Washita Jolly, care of Judge Isaac Parker's Court, Fort Smith, Arkansas." Jolly's eyes searched Drake's face. "You got that?"

"I'm not likely to forget."

"Don't, or I'll come looking for you."

"Washita," Luke said, his face empty, "you got a heart of gold."

"I know that." The deputy sighed. "It's my only weakness."

Drake stood beside the graying embers of the dying fire. He'd been there for some time.

Jolly and his prisoners had pulled out an hour before, just as the dawn brightened into morning, and since then Drake had been lost in thought.

He told himself he had three choices, but in reality he only had one.

Without Withers, he couldn't ride into Green Meadow, where he'd surely be shot on sight, and torture and death awaited him at the Fat Man's camp.

The only course left to him was to ride away and leave all this far behind him. He could point the gray mustang south and not draw rein until he reached Texas.

A one-handed man could always find work. It didn't take two hands to swamp a saloon or draw water and pitch hay in a livery stable.

A terrible tiredness in him, Drake felt done, used up.

Even the vision of Harvey Thornton at the end of his gun barrel did nothing to energize him.

Sometimes a man reaches a realization about a thing, and he knows there's no stepping away from it. He can only accept what is thrown at him.

He'd gotten in the way of them all, the good and the bad, the Fat Man, John D. Rockefeller, Karl Benz, Helen Lee, all of them moneyed and powerful, and they'd squashed him like a bug.

Mutilated, penniless, wearing a dead man's clothes and a hat that came down to the top of his ears, Drake knew he was beaten.

He rode the gray mustang out of the trees and onto the flat, head hanging, chin on his chest.

Like a whipped dog, he told himself.

And he knew that, for as long as he lived, he would never again be able to hold his head high in the company of men.

Chapter 33

Often a man meets his fate on the very road he takes to avoid it, and so it happened with Chauncey Drake.

He crossed Rock Creek where it arcs among the foothills of Red Oak Mountain to the west, Red Oak Peak to the east. Riding into the gap between the buttes, after thirty minutes the wagon road between Green Meadow and Wilburton appeared, straight as a string, to the south.

Even at a distance, the pair of riders on the road seemed familiar. Alert now, like a predator scenting prey, Drake rode closer.

Now there was no mistaking them.

The two men, both riding paint horses, had been part of the bunch that had been with Thornton.

They'd had fun. Drake remembered that.

He felt anger scorch his belly like a hot coal.

Mild-mannered people say a man should never get angry, that it's a destructive force that resides only in the bosom of fools. But Drake harnessed his rage, used it to shed his self-pity and sense of helplessness.

The sight of men who had whipped him with ropes and laughed at his pain and humiliation set his teeth on edge . . . and filled him with a terrible resolve.

"Withers," he said, "this is for you."

He said it only to himself, but hoped that somewhere, somehow, the little Pinkerton was listening.

The riders were coming from the west, and Drake angled across two hundred yards of open ground, intending to cut them off.

But the men stopped and one of them turned, stood in his stirrups, and scouted his back trail, hat raised to shade his eyes from the climbing sun.

Intent on what they were doing, Thornton's men hadn't even seen Drake draw close.

He reached the road and slowed the mustang to a walk.

Now they were aware of him and they both turned to face him.

Drake rode within ten yards of the pair, then drew rein.

"Howdy, boys," he said. "Remember me?"

The younger of the riders, a redhead with freckles across the bridge of his nose and reckless eyes, gave Drake the once-over and said, "Who the hell are you? We don't recollect every saddle tramp we come across."

"This help?"

Drake held up his left hand, covered in a blood-soaked bandage.

Now they recognized him, and saw something in his eyes and the stiff set of his shoulders that gave them pause.

"Hell, boy, we was only funnin'," the older man said.

"Yeah, that's it, only funnin'," the redhead said. "Now give us the road."

Drake had not lowered his hand. "Is this your idea of a joke?"

As a rule, professional gunfighters were a canny breed. They fought for profit, and would not unnecessarily risk their lives merely to build reputations as hard cases.

The men facing Drake knew there was little to be gained by shooting it out with a shabby saddle tramp riding a ten-dollar horse. But they would not be pushed, and now Drake was pushing them hard, his anger seething.

"You're a couple of low-life tinhorns," he said. "And I mean to leave both of you dead on the trail."

Still the gunmen would not draw.

"Go sleep it off, boy," the older man said. "We got twenty men coming right behind us, so count yourself lucky that all you've lost is your fingers."

"You going to skin iron, or do I have to shoot you down like the pair of mangy yellow dogs you are?" Drake said.

It was war talk, and way more than the young redhead was willing to take.

He went for his gun.

And Drake shot him.

The older man was bug-eyed, unpleasantly surprised at Drake's speed. It slowed him by a half second, maybe less, and it killed him.

His Colt hadn't cleared leather when Drake's second bullet slammed into him high in the chest.

The redhead, hit hard in the belly, had bent over his gun and his horse was giving him trouble. But he got off a shot that burned Drake across the left cheek and another that missed.

The mustang, outlaw trained, stood foursquare, a rock-steady gun platform.

Drake fired at the redhead, saw his bullet hit, fired again. Another hit.

This time the man raised himself in the stirrups, his face ashen, and crashed to the ground.

The older rider was still mounted, staring in horror and disbelief at Drake. But there was no fight left in him, blood making a scarlet O of his mouth.

"You," he said, "a . . . a . . . draw fighter."

"Seems like," Drake said. "Surprised the hell out of my own self."

He raised his Colt, thumbed back the hammer, and drew a bead. He shot the gunman in the middle of the forehead, just under his hatband. The man threw up his hands and toppled off his horse.

His eyes on the trail to the west, Drake reloaded, then slid the Colt back into the leather.

A dust cloud was kicking up less than half a mile away, a large body of men coming on at a gallop.

Without sparing a glance for the two dead men sprawled on the trail, Drake swung the mustang north again and headed for the valley between the mountains.

He smiled to himself. He'd fought back for the first time.

And it felt good.

Chapter 34

Chauncey Drake cleared the buttes and swung west, heading for the wooded foothills of the Sans Bois. Behind him two dozen riders fanned out across the flat, firing rifles as they came.

But these were the gun hands the Fat Man had brought up from Texas. They were close-up fighters who did not earn their wages for their skills with a rifle. Most of their fire went wide, but one or two bullets split the air uncomfortably close to Drake's head.

The mustang was showing a remarkable turn of speed and the little horse had plenty of bottom.

Drake had been fooled by the gray's ugly hammer head and runty size, but now, running for his life on the flat, he understood why it had been an outlaw's mount.

Ahead of Drake two low hills bordered a dry wash. He plunged into the gap and followed the wash until it opened up into a rise studded with juniper, cactus, and a few stunted cottonwoods.

He stole a fast glance over his shoulder.

The Texans were still coming, closer now, firing, and Drake cursed under his breath. One of the men he'd killed must surely be somebody back there's kin.

The mustang took the rise in stride, but Drake was wearing out fast.

Weak from loss of blood, his head spun, nausea curled in his belly, and his breath came in short, sharp gasps.

As he crested the rise, he leaned sideways in the saddle and tried to throw up, but produced only a string of saliva that bent like a bow, then blew away in the wind.

Before Drake had a chance to straighten, the mustang hit the trees at a gallop. The little horse had aimed for a gap between two tall hickories, but a lower branch thumped into Drake's chest and swept him from the saddle.

He lay stunned for few moments, then struggled to a sitting position, his head reeling.

It dawned on him that he was very vulnerable. Thornton's riders could be on top of him at any moment.

It took a great effort of will, but Drake got to his feet and pulled his gun. He backed up to the hickory, determined to sell his life dearly.

But the hundred yards of flat ground that came off the rise and ended at the trees was empty. There was no sound, no movement.

Drake wiped dirt and saliva from his mouth with the back of his gun hand and waited.

A pair of fox squirrels played chase among the branches of the hickory, raining down a shower of dry leaves and bark. To the west, a red-tailed hawk rode the air currents, mouse-hunting with eyes as large as a man's.

Leaving the tree, his Colt ready, Drake walked across the flat to the edge of the rise.

The Texans were gone, riding in a column to the north, in the direction of the Fat Man's camp.

Drake sighed his relief. If they'd caught him a few minutes earlier, he'd be a dead man by now.

He'd no explanation for why Thornton had called off the chase and he didn't ponder it too deeply. The obvious answer was that the gunman had more pressing business at hand—the attack on Green Meadow.

When Drake returned to the trees, the mustang stood a few yards away among some oaks, head lowered, dozing.

All the charitable feelings Drake had for the horse evaporated. The damned hammer head had come close to getting him killed.

"Come here, you," he said, picking up the reins. "And don't even look at me for the rest of the day."

The mustang didn't seem contrite, didn't seem anything, as Drake led it to the bottom of the ridge and mounted.

His gunfight with the two gunmen had changed him. In less than fifteen seconds he'd gone from a pathetic hunted creature to a dangerous avenger, and the transformation sat well with him.

He had more wrongs to right and he vowed to himself that he would never again fail the test. No matter what happened, from this day onward, he would hold his head high.

What he needed now was food and rest, and the

only place he could hope to find either was the Waterses'
cabin. It was an ill-fated, haunted place, to be sure,
and probably picked clean by now, but it was his only
option.

The cabin on Rock Creek seemed the same as before.
The only changes were the weeds that grew in the window boxes and the barn door leaning aslant on its bottom
hinge.

But two things troubled Drake as he sat his horse
and studied the place.

One was the shadow he saw pass in front of a smashed
window, the other the ribbon of smoke that rose from
the chimney and tied bows in the breeze.

Someone was inside. It was unlikely to be any of
Thornton's men, more likely a puncher riding the grub
line and passing through.

Drake swung out of the saddle, then drew his gun.

There was one way to find out.

Chapter 35

Drake knew he was in no shape for another fight, but he did not sense any immediate danger.

He advanced on the cabin, his eyes constantly moving between the two front windows. Nothing stirred inside, though once he thought he heard the thud of a boot heel on the wood floor.

The cabin door was slightly ajar, and Drake took advantage of someone's carelessness. He raised his boot and kicked it open, diving inside as the door's thin timbers splintered against the wall.

"Don't shoot, mister!"

An old man jumped up from a chair and flattened himself against the wall, his hands grabbing air above his head.

"It's only me, mister, poor ol' Silas Gust as ever was!"

Behind him, Drake heard a sharp intake of breath. His nerves shredding, he spun around, his gun leveling.

A young girl in a pink gingham dress stood in the doorway to the bedroom, a hand to her throat.

"Damn it, I could have shot you," he said.

"Leave her be," Gust said. "She's only an orphan child."

Drake waved the Colt. "Get over there beside your pappy, and don't ever sneak up on a man again."

There was defiance in the tilt of the girl's chin and the stiffness of her back, but she did as Drake had ordered.

"I don't sneak," she said as she took her place beside the old man.

"Don't sass me, girl," Drake said. He looked at Gust. "What are you doing here?"

"We needed shelter and the cabin was empty," the old man said. "Do you own the place, mister?"

"No, I don't. The owners are dead."

"I know that," the girl said. "I've seen the woman standing right where you are, all pale and sad." She smiled. "I'm wearing one of her dresses, but she didn't seem to mind."

Ghosts and ha'ants were things Drake could not abide and he felt a shiver run along his spine. But his face was locked down tight as he holstered his gun and said to Gust, "Put your hands down, old-timer. I'm not going to shoot you, at least not right now."

"Thankee, sonny," Gust said, dropping his arms. "For a minute there you worried the hell out of me."

Drake lifted his nose. "The coffee smells good."

"I'll get you some," the girl said.

Drake dropped into a chair and the old man sat opposite him.

"I didn't catch your name, mister," Gust said.

"Maybe because I didn't give it. Name's Chauncey Drake."

"Right pleased to meet you, Chauncey. I'm Silas. The girl is Nancy."

Nancy brought Drake a steaming cup. It was only then she saw the stained bandage on his left hand.

"What happened to you?" she said.

"Got my fingers shot off," Drake said, gratefully drinking the hot, strong coffee.

"I need to take a look at that hand," Nancy said.

Gust had been studying Drake with shrewd blue eyes.

"You on the scout, Chauncey?" he asked.

Drake smiled. "Seems like the whole territory is after me."

"Want to talk about it? I'm too old for much, but I'm an advising man."

"Maybe later. Maybe not."

"Suit yourself. Talk is cheap, anyhow."

"When did you last eat?" Nancy asked.

Gust cackled. "Now there's a question a man gets only from womenfolk."

"I can't remember," Drake said. "It's been a spell."

"I'll fix you something."

"You don't need to trouble yourself."

"No trouble. I like to see a man eat."

Nancy had dark eyes, dark hair, and was very pretty. Drake thought she looked to be about sixteen, but she could have been younger.

As the girl busied herself at the stove, he said to Gust, "You told me the girl is an orphan, so she isn't kin. How did you two meet up?"

"I found her."

"Found her? Where?"

"Down south a ways, west of Dutchman Ridge. I

was prospecting and first come across her when she walked into my camp."

Gust shook his head. "She was a poorly looking little thing, dressed in rags and all battered and bruised. Said she was running from a farmer who had treated her bad."

"He enjoyed beating me," Nancy said, turning her head from the stove to look at Drake. "And he"—she was searching for words—"came at me all the time with his . . . thing. Finally I waited until one night when he was too drunk to stand and ran away."

"That was a month ago, and we've been on the scout ever since," Gust said.

"What do you mean, on the scout?"

"Hell, Chauncey, he came after us," Gust said. "He wants his slave girl back. When you came a-bustin' through the door, I thought fer sure you was him." The old man shook his head. "An' me with my rifle over to the door. I ain't never gonna leave it there again."

"What's he like, this sodbuster?"

"Big man, has mean eyes and a red beard down to his belt buckle. And he's right handy with a rifle. Took a shot at me down Blue Mountain way and came damn close to blowin' out my candle permanent."

Nancy brought a plate and fork to the table and laid them in front of Drake.

"Eggs fried in bacon grease and some of Silas's sour-dough bread," she said.

"Stick to your ribs, boy," the old man said. "You're way too skinny anyhow."

Drake ate like a starving man, Nancy watching his every bite with smiling approval.

It surprised Drake that he found himself liking the girl, liking her a lot.

And with that dawned the realization that Nancy came with a price—he would acquire another dangerous enemy.

Chapter 36

"You just sit there and let Nancy take care of that hand, Chauncey," Gust said. "Them potions of hers worked wonders on my rheumatisms."

The girl was gently spreading a salve on the raw stumps of Drake's fingers, her pretty face frowning in concentration.

"How come you know this stuff?" Drake asked.

"My ma was a swamp witch—that was what she called herself. Told me she was born and raised in a Louisiana bayou, and she showed me what herbs heal, and them that don't."

"What happened to her?"

"She died."

"Of what?"

"I don't know. One day after Pa was killed by a runaway mule, she lay in bed, turned her face to the wall, and just died. Couldn't live without Pa, I guess."

"Takes a black-eyed woman to be a swamp witch," Gust said.

"Eyes like mine," Nancy said.

"Is that why you see dead people?" Drake said, smiling. "On account of your ma being a swamp witch an' all?"

"That's why. What's bred in the bone comes out in the marrow."

"You see dead people a lot?"

"All the time."

"You see any right now?"

"Just one—a man who's going to get killed if he doesn't keep his hand still."

Drake laughed and it felt just fine.

Later, his stumps freshly bandaged and a lot of the hurt gone, Drake shared a jug with Gust, letting the old man talk.

"Being a prospector all my born days, I haven't been around farmers much," Gust said, "but the sodbuster who owned this farm never threw away anything in his life. Have you seen his barn?"

Drake had seen too much of the Waterses' barn, but he shook his head. "Can't say as I have."

"He's got everything in there he ever owned, bits of broken harness, old rusty nails, wire, dynamite, pieces of scrap wood, you name it. Why, he even has—"

Drake sat up in his chair. "What did you say, Silas?"

"Huh? About what?"

"You said dynamite. Is there still dynamite in the barn?"

"Sure is, a box full of the stuff. And it's old."

"Have you ever used dynamite?"

"Yeah, plenty of times. I'm a placer miner, but I've done my share of blastin' in the past."

Gust took his pipe from his mouth. "What's your drift?"

"Silas, I think Chauncey is a man with a story to tell," Nancy said.

Drake took a pull on the jug, then told it.

After Drake finished talking, a silence stretched, tense as a fiddle string.

Head lowered, Gust filled his pipe and Nancy's stare went to the window as though she'd suddenly seen something of great interest out in the darkening afternoon.

"You don't believe me, either of you," Drake said.

Gust raised his faded eyes. "We believe you, sonny. You got no reason to lie to poor folks like us."

"I can't stop the Fat Man's attack on Green Meadow," Drake said. "But I can use the dynamite to slow him up some."

"How? How you going to do that?" Gust said.

"I was hoping you'd show me."

"Wrong answer. Any dang fool can light a stick of dynamite. Getting it to where it will do the most good is another matter."

"Connect the fuses, or whatever it is you do to make dynamite bang, and I'll handle the rest."

"You mean to throw it, don't you, boy?"

"Something like that."

"Close-up work, throwing dynamite, and mighty dangerous. You got the hoss fer it?"

"I don't understand."

"When dynamite goes off next to a hoss that can't handle loud noises, he'll buck an' run and leave you flat on your ass."

"My horse can handle it. He's handled everything else."

Nancy shook her head. "It's too dangerous, Chauncey. Silas and me will go to Green Meadow with you. They might listen to us."

Gust shook his head. "A crazy old coot of a failed prospector and a poor orphan girl with witch eyes? They ain't gonna listen to us, Nancy. We ain't exactly what you might call gentry. Besides . . ."

Gust took time to relight his pipe, the lengthy ritual that pipe smokers much enjoy.

"Besides," he said finally, "part of what Chauncey told us ain't exactly the truth."

Drake opened his mouth to object, but Gust held up a hand to silence him.

"I'm not calling you a liar, sonny," he said. "But somebody is lying."

Irritated, Drake said, "What part of my story do you reckon is a lie?"

"All that talk about the oil. At one time or another, I've prospected all over these parts, from the Sans Bois to Limestone Ridge, and never once come up on a tar seep."

"What's that, Silas?" Nancy said.

"Well, oil and tar bubble to the surface and form a pool they call a seep. Down Texas way, the Comanche used tar to waterproof their canteens and the twine around their lance heads. The women balled up tar and used it as weights to hold down their skirts and to cement broken pots and the like."

The old man nodded. "Yup the Indians used tar and oil for a lot of stuff." He smiled at Drake. "Only there's none of it around here."

"So if there's no seeps, there's no oil?" Drake asked.

"It ain't likely."

"But how could Rockefeller be so sure there was oil here?" Drake said.

"He's an oilman, Chauncey. He must know there's plenty of oil in the Oklahoma Territory, but not around this neck of the woods."

Drake looked out the shattered window where the light was fleeing the darkness.

"Then all the murders, the people in Green Meadow, they'll die because somebody is lying."

"Or because somebody messed up, claiming there's oil where none exists," Gust said. "Your Pinkerton friend maybe." He puffed on his pipe. "Or the damned government."

Chapter 37

Chauncey Drake rose from his chair and paced restlessly to the window, his mind reeling.

He stared into the gloom and for a few moments listened to the whisper of the wind and the coyotes yipping close to the farm, hunting stray chickens.

Then, in a moment of awful clarity, Drake understood, or at least began to understand, what had happened.

Could it be that President Harrison had called in favors and asked John D. Rockefeller, even the German Karl Benz, to set up the Fat Man, with Pinkerton help? But had they all failed because they'd badly underestimated the man's cunning and ruthlessness?

The Fat Man had never met with Rockefeller and Benz, never did anything by word or deed to incriminate himself. Drake himself had been part of his strategy to shift blame if anything went wrong.

But, worried that Rockefeller was distancing himself from the deal, the Fat Man realized that a fortune was slipping through his fingers. Desperate, he was gambling all on one last throw of the dice—an attack on Green Meadow.

Rockefeller was unaware of the Fat Man's plan, and so was President Harrison. As a result, hundreds of people were about to die . . . for oil that didn't exist.

The more Drake considered it, the more he was sure he'd hit on the reason for the phantom oil. The Fat Man was an enemy of the state, but they could not bring him down by legal means.

Setting him up so he could trip himself and fall seemed like a reasonable option.

"It's the government, I tell ye, Chauncey," Gust said. "They never get anything right in Washington."

Drake nodded, then turned and looked at Gust. "There are only a few people who know about the Fat Man's planned attack, and three of them are right here in this room."

"And what does that tell us?" Gust said.

"It tells us we're the only ones who can stop it."

"Chauncey, you owe Green Meadow nothing, the way it treated you," Nancy said.

"A town isn't just buildings and businesses, Nancy. It's people—the men, women, and children who live in it. I can't turn my back on them and still consider myself a man."

"No, you can't, Chauncey, not hardly," Gust said, nodding. "I'm with you there."

"Chauncey, you haven't slept and you're weak from loss of blood," Nancy said. "You can't go up against fifty gunmen. You'll just get yourself killed, like all the rest."

She dropped her eyes, her lashes lying like black

fans on her cheekbones. "We met only today, but . . . there's something." She looked at Drake. "I care about you."

Nancy turned and ran into the bedroom, slamming the creaking door behind her.

"She's taken a shine to you, boy." Gust grinned.

"I like her too," Drake said.

Gust sat back in his chair and found his pipe. "Ah, well," he said, "I'm an advising man, but I'm too old to advise you on love stuff."

Drake rubbed the stubble on his cheeks and chin.

"Silas, do you have a razor? If I'm about to meet my Maker, I want to stand before Him clean-shaven."

"Six sticks, Chauncey, ready to go," Gust said. "But it's old stuff and maybe damp."

"After I light the fuse on a stick, how long do I have before it bangs?"

"Are you a praying man, boy?"

"No. But I recollect some."

"Good, so say, 'The Lord is my shepherd, I shall not want.' That's how long you got. Them are mighty short fuses."

"Damned plowboy liked to live dangerously, didn't he?" Drake said.

"Seems like. But then, a man who cheats on his wife lives dangerously even without dynamite."

Gust stepped to the barn door and looked outside.

"Wish I could come with you, boy," he said. "But me and my old mule would only slow you down."

"It's going to be fast, Silas. One ride through the camp and then I'm out of there."

The old man shook his head. "Studying on it. She's thin, Chauncey, mighty thin."

"I'll hit them just before sunup, when men are in their deepest sleep. Before they realize what's happening, I'll be gone."

For a moment, Drake looked stricken, patting his pockets. "Hell, I almost forgot about matches."

Gust sighed. "Chauncey, I don't have a good feeling about this. You danged sure you want to handle dynamite?"

"I can handle it. When it comes down to actually doing the thing, I'll handle it."

"How?"

"What do you mean, how? It isn't difficult."

"With one mitt it is."

Later, studying on it, Drake blamed fear for his mental lapse. He hadn't even considered how a one-handed man lights a stick of dynamite until Gust questioned him on it.

Now the old man echoed his own thoughts.

"You maybe going to hold the dynamite in your teeth?" Gust cackled. "Blow your damn fool head off, Chauncey."

"I'll manage it. A man wants to do a thing badly enough, he'll find a way."

"Right, well, here's what you do: The sodbuster left a cigar in the bedroom, dried out, which is more than I can say for the dynamite. Fire up the cigar, then use it to light the fuses. And by that I mean, hold the cigar in your teeth, not the dynamite."

Looking at Drake with worried eyes, he said, "You remember all that?"

"Yeah."

"What prayer do you say, boy?"

Drake smiled. "I'll remember it. Now bring the cigar. I don't want to go back into the cabin and wake Nancy."

"She ain't sleeping, Chauncey. She's even more worried than I am my own self. How's the hand?"

"I can still feel the fingers and they hurt like hell."

"Heard o' that, but usually it's, like, a missing arm or leg."

Drake stepped to the barn door and looked outside.

A waning moon rode high and a million stars roofed the lilac night. The air smelled of pine and of shadowed, musty places where green frogs climbed among ferns.

"Better bring the cigar soon, Silas," he said. "The coward half of me wants to forget the whole shebang and hide out with you and Nancy in the cabin."

Gust nodded. "To see the right and not do it is cowardice, boy. To see the right and do it, no matter how scared you are, that's having sand."

"Cut-and-dried choice, ain't it, Silas?"

"Yup, and a man can only choose for himself."

After a while Drake said, "Get the damned cigar."

Chapter 38

Drake swung into the saddle, then hesitated as Nancy left the cabin and walked toward him.

Before Drake could speak, the girl said, "Chauncey, step down. I'll settle for the coward half of you."

"Silas told you, huh?"

"You're throwing your life away."

"I'll be back, Nancy. For the first time in my life, I have someone to come home to."

"And me."

"Happened quick, didn't it?"

"I guess that's how it goes sometimes."

"I got to be on my way."

"Is there nothing I can say that will make you change your mind?"

"Just looking at you standing with the moonlight all tangled up in your hair makes me want to change my mind." Drake smiled. "That's why I got to go. Now, before I weaken any further."

"You don't have to be brave for me, Chauncey. Is it such a bad thing to be a coward?"

"Nancy, you already know the answer to that. And I'm not being brave. I'm scared to death."

"Then stay. I need you, Chauncey, and so does Silas."

"I have got to go, Nancy."

"Then there's nothing more to say?"

"Just wish me luck."

"Death rides with you, Chauncey. I can see him plain, grinning at me."

"Nancy! You let the man go!"

Gust emerged from the darkness.

"He don't need a black-eyed witch woman telling him about death. He can see him clear his own self."

Drake swallowed hard. "I'll be back."

As he rode away he heard two sounds, Nancy's sobs and Gust saying, "Don't forget to say your prayer, boy."

Drake waved his hand, but the old man didn't see it.

Drake followed Rock Creek into the Sans Bois foot-hills, trusting to moonlight and the mustang to find the way.

When he reached the arroyo that led to the clearing he calculated it was still two hours shy of daybreak. The moon had dropped lower in the sky but the hills were silvered, floating in pools of shadow.

Drake stepped out of the saddle and dropped the mustang's reins.

The last time he'd passed this way there had been a sentry at the end of the gulch. He didn't know if it was still guarded, but he couldn't take a chance on it being otherwise.

Drake climbed the slope of the arroyo onto a rim covered with juniper and wild oak. The ground underfoot was mostly grass, but here and there were patches of limestone shingle and rock.

On cat feet, he made his way between the trees, following a little-used game trail, careful to avoid places where his boots would crunch on gravel. After a couple of minutes he came up on a group of boulders and got down on his knees among them.

More tired than he'd ever thought possible, Drake rested, listening into the darkness. The wind rustled in the trees and from somewhere close by, among the pines, an owl asked his question of the night.

His mouth powder dry, heart thumping, Drake rose from the rocks and made his way forward. After a couple of steps a twig snapped under his boot heel and he froze, the hair on the back of his neck rising.

For long moments, Drake stood like a statue, expecting a shouted challenge, or worse, a bullet.

Neither came.

The wind whispered as before, the owl had not ceased its insistent questioning, and the night was still whole.

Drake rubbed a sweaty palm on his pants and stayed where he was, waiting until his heart beat slower. After a minute he drew his Colt, grateful for its cold assurance, and walked on . . . into disaster.

"Stand right there, mister."

The voice came from Drake's left.

His options limited, he spun around and fired.

An instant later a bullet cracked past his head.

Now Drake saw his target, a man standing half in shadow. He fired again. This time he scored a hit. The man staggered, levering his rifle at thigh level. Too slow.

Drake fired, fired a second time. Riding the last bullet into hell, the man rose up on tiptoes and crashed onto his face.

His fatigue forgotten, Drake ran. He scrambled down the slope of the arroyo and sprinted for his horse. Behind him he heard the dazed shouts of wakening men and guns being fired at phantoms.

Drake ran to the mustang, took a couple sticks of dynamite from his saddlebags, and tucked them into his shirt. He'd stashed the cigar under his hat, and now he stuck it between his lips and tried to thumb a match into flame.

He was shaking badly and the match head broke.

The yelling was getting closer, and lights bobbed at the end of the arroyo as men held high flaming brands from the fires.

Drake tried another match. This time he managed to get the cigar lit, puffing at it frantically to encourage its cherry red coal.

He took a stick of dynamite from his shirt, held the fuse to the glowing end of the cigar. The black powder sputtered and smoked; then a red ant of fire scuttled along the fuse toward the stick.

"Mine eyes have seen the glory . . ."

He was saying the wrong damned prayer!

Drake cursed and threw the dynamite as far as he could, aiming for the top of the ridge to his left.

The resulting explosion was all that he could have hoped for.

The crest of the rim erupted in a gigantic column of fire and smoke. A wild oak rose high in the air and crashed into the arroyo, followed by a shattering shower of shingle.

"Yeeee-haw!" Drake yelled, grinning, his pain and tiredness forgotten, like men before him and since, awed by the power of giant powder.

He lit another stick and tossed it. Again the result was a gratifying *boom* of uprooted trees and thumping rock.

Bullets clipped the air around Drake and rifles flared on the rim opposite. Despite the crash of the explosions, the mustang had held steady. Head hanging, the little horse seemed oblivious to what was happening around it.

Drake swung into the saddle and galloped from the arroyo. Bullets chased him, but none came close.

After a few minutes he slowed to a trot and let the mustang pick its way, riding under a brightening sky with only a few sentinel stars still awake.

As his euphoria thinned, Drake understood he'd accomplished little.

It would take only a couple of hours to clear the arroyo. He'd slowed the Fat Man only by that long.

It had been Drake's intention to make a slow circuit of the clearing, then launch his charge, keeping his last stick of dynamite for the Fat Man's cabin—if he'd lived long enough to get that far.

Blocking the arroyo had been his second-best effort, and not near good enough.

But just maybe his puny demonstration had made the Fat Man cautious. Caution is the nagging wife of action, and he could have no idea who made the attack. That uncertainty might slow him.

And I could be pissing into the wind, Drake thought, gloom coming down on him.

Chapter 39

"Well, what do you think?" Drake said.

"I reckon he'll keep on coming and do what he wants to do," Gust said.

"The question is when? Today? Tomorrow? How long does Green Meadow have to live?"

There was no answer to that question and Gust was silent.

Nancy stepped into the quiet.

"Chauncey, you have to sleep," she said. "You're dead on your feet."

"I have to think," Drake said. "That's what I have to do."

"A tired man doesn't think well. Sleep for a few hours and you'll see things clearer."

"What's clear, Nancy, is that I can't stand idly by and let the Fat Man destroy the town."

"Nancy's right, boy," Gust said. "Get some sleep. Then we'll all study on it. Maybe we'll come up with an answer pretty quick."

Drake had no confidence in what the old man said.

But he was exhausted and right now sleep was his obvious option.

Nancy saw him weaken.

"Lie on the bed, Chauncey," she said. "I'll take your boots off."

"A few hours, no more than that," Drake said, rising from his chair.

He later recalled walking into the bedroom and throwing himself on the bed. He vaguely remembered Nancy pulling off his boots, but he would not remember falling asleep.

Drake dreamed of gunfire, smoke, and the screams of dying men.

Had he wakened and asked Nancy what the dreams portended, she would have told him another killing and more blood.

But he slept on, and the dream would remain unfulfilled . . . until he woke.

The raised voices outside wakened Drake.

He had no idea if he'd slept ten minutes or ten hours, but the day was still bright, beams of sunlight hazed with dust streaming through the bedroom window.

Outside a man's voice, harsh and hard on the ear, climbed into a shout.

"You're coming with me, you little bitch. And when I get you back to the farm, I'll horsewhip the tar out of ye."

Drake rose. He awkwardly swung his gun belt around his hips, a difficult task for a one-handed man. He gave up, tossed the belt on the bed and drew the Colt.

On bare feet he padded to the door, and then hesitated, letting his swimming head steady, listening.

"Nancy ain't going with you, mister, not now, not ever."

It was Gust's voice, harder than Drake had ever heard it.

"I paid twenty dollars for the sow and I have a bill of sale. I'm taking back what's legally mine, old man."

"Sodbuster, this here Henry rifle gun says you ain't."

There was a silence.

Then the farmer spoke again. "I'll be back, and I'll bring the law with me."

"Suit yourself," Gust said.

Drake heard the hoof falls of a retreating horse.

A blind panic seized him.

An angry man doesn't give up that easily!

Drake opened the door and yelled Gust's name. He stepped outside as the farmer wheeled and set spurs to his horse, his rifle coming up fast to his shoulder.

Surprised, Gust hesitated a moment.

Drake raised his Colt. Nancy ran in front of his gun, trying to shield Gust, and Drake yelled at her to get away.

The sodbuster's rifle roared and Gust stepped back, hit.

The old man steadied, worked his rifle from the hip, and fired. The big red-bearded man reeled in the saddle.

Drake fired, missing the man who was already toppling from his horse. The farmer hit the ground in a cloud of dust, rolled, and lay still.

Gust thumped onto his butt and looked at Drake. "Did you get your work in, Chauncey?"

"Missed him."

"Is he dead?"

"His bullet put you in bed, old-timer. Your bullet put him in the grave."

"Serves him right. I could never abide a red-bearded man anyhow. It ain't natural."

Nancy knelt beside Gust. She gently pushed the old man onto his back.

"Nancy, I can't feel my left leg. Is that where I'm hit?"

The girl examined Gust's leg. She looked at Drake. "I think he's got a bullet in his thigh."

"Let me take a look," Drake said.

He carefully rolled Gust onto his side and the old man winced.

"Easy, easy, old-timer," Drake said.

He looked the leg over. "Bullet went all the way through. I don't think it hit bone."

"Chauncey, he's bleeding, bleeding a lot."

"Damn it, girl, I'm here," Gust said. "Tell me, not him."

"We're getting you inside, Silas," Nancy said. "I have to stop the bleeding."

A pool of blood had formed under Gust, and there was more coming.

Drake didn't like the look of it. He'd once seen a man bleed out on the floor of a saloon after getting a knife in the brisket and the amount of blood had been a lot less then.

Nancy and Drake carried Gust inside and laid the old man on the floor and the girl brought a pillow for his head.

After an hour, a sheet from the bed lay wadded beside Nancy, a sodden, crimson testimony to a man who was slowly bleeding to death.

Gust was very pale and blue shadows had gathered under his eyes and in the hollows of his cheeks.

He looked at Drake with eyes that could no longer focus. "Damned sodbuster done for me, huh, Chauncey?"

Drake's gaze met Nancy's. He saw grief, pain, and nothing of hope.

"Seems like, old-timer," Drake said.

"Well, I'll buy him a drink in hell, for old time's sake, like."

Gust tried to find Nancy in the darkness that was closing in on him.

"Nancy?"

"I'm here, Silas. Close."

"You heard o' Stephen Foster?"

Nancy shook her head, then realized that Gust could no longer see her. "I don't know him, Silas."

"He wrote a song by the name of 'Beautiful Dreamer.' Sing it fer me, Nancy. I reckon I'm about ready to follow the buffalo herd somewheres."

"Silas," Nancy said, her voice breaking, "I don't know any songs."

Drake had heard Stephen Foster tunes performed in a hundred saloons and he knew and liked "Beautiful Dreamer."

"Silas, I can sing it for you," he said. "That is, if my voice is to your liking."

"Let me hear it, boy. Sing it real pretty, now."

Beautiful dreamer, wake unto me,
Starlight and dewdrops are waiting for thee;
Sounds of the rude world heard in the day,
Lulled by the moonlight have all passed away.

Gust's voice, a faint whisper, joined with Drake's fine tenor.

Beautiful dreamer, queen of my song,
List while I woo thee with soft melody;
Gone are the cares of life's busy throng,
Beautiful Dreamer, awake unto me,
Beautiful Dreamer, awake unto me.

Silas Gust's voice faltered and died, his life ending with the song.

"He's gone," Nancy said through tears.

Drake nodded. "He had sand, and he was true blue. Splendid behavior."

"Is that all we have to say about him?" Nancy said.

"It's better than what's said about most men."

The girl rose to her feet and stepped to the door, her face stiff, desolate.

Drake followed her outside in time to see Nancy pick up Gust's Henry.

The girl stepped to the dead farmer and pumped bullet after bullet into his body, tears streaming down her cheeks.

Drake crossed the yard and took the empty rifle from her hands.

"I want to bring the son of a bitch back to life and kill him all over again," Nancy said. "And do it over and over, until he suffered like Silas did."

Drake pulled the girl close to him. "Silas didn't suffer, Nancy. He died game and without pain."

Nancy buried her face in Drake's chest, her shuddering sobs so long and loud that he feared she would never stop.

Chapter 40

Drake saddled up the mustang, threw a loop around the farmer's neck, and dragged the body into the woods away from the house.

By the time he returned, Nancy had washed Gust and covered him with a clean sheet. Now she stood lonely vigil beside his body, her head bowed, face still.

Earlier they had laid him out on the table and now the old man looked shrunken under the sheet, as though his departed spirit had taken half of him with it.

Drake found the jug and poured whiskey into a cup. He offered it to the girl. "Drink this. It will help."

Nancy did not turn or acknowledge him. Her tears had stopped, but she stood as still and unmoving as the grave itself.

Drake had neither the words nor the practiced ease around women that come so easily to many men. He sat on a chair, watching the girl, sipping on the fiery rye, grateful for its bite.

An hour passed, then another. Nancy had not moved or made a sound.

Finally Drake rose. As he passed her, he laid his hand on her shoulder. She neither accepted his clumsy comfort nor pulled away. Nancy was in a secret place where she could be alone with her grief, and there was no bringing her back.

The day was well gone as Drake stepped outside.

As far as the eye could see, the sky was a fragile blue, ready to shatter into a million pieces and fall to earth as splinters of moonlight. A drowsy wind from the south, heavy with pine and sage, smelled fragrant as a beautiful woman's hair.

On his way to the barn, Drake stopped, enjoying the waning day, its quiet lying on the land like a blessing.

He thought of Silas, cold as marble, his days in the sun over. And it filled him with a sadness and a sense of wonder that he could grieve for anyone.

The barn was slanted with shadow, the dead farmer's sorrel chomping on the last of the hay. The mustang seemed disinterested as ever, dozing on his feet, a cloud of flies droning around his head.

Drake stood, lost in thought. The Fat Man's attack on Green Meadow could come at any time—and all he could do about it was stand in a barn and look at an ugly horse.

There had to be—

"Turn around easy, Mr. Drake."

The woman's voice came from behind him.

Drake's Colt was tucked into the waistband of his pants, handy enough for the draw and shoot. But turning, then finding his target, would slow him.

The woman read his mind.

"Mr. Drake, if I see anything that gives me alarm, I'll drop you."

The voice was familiar.

"Fancy meeting you here, Miss Lee," Drake said.

He turned slowly to face the woman.

Helen Lee no longer looked like the fashionable belle he'd met in Green Meadow. Her face was streaked with mud, her hair matted, tangled with leaves and tree bark, and her split riding skirt and shirt were stained from hard use.

But the Webley & Scott Bulldog revolver in her hand was clean and the muzzle didn't waver a fraction, aimed right at Drake's belly.

"Was it you at the gulch?" Helen Lee asked.

"Yes."

"You played hob."

"I tried to."

"Four men dead and a couple more missing limbs."

Drake was surprised. "How did that happen?"

"Could it be that it's because you blew them up with dynamite?"

"I figured I'd toppled a few trees, nothing more."

"Figured wrong, didn't you, Mr. Drake?"

"Did you come here to take me back?"

"Hardly. After you started to blow up everything in sight, I escaped in the confusion. The Fat Man wasn't going to let me leave his camp alive."

"Are they coming after you?"

"I don't know, probably. I do know I can't stay here. It's the first place they'll look."

Helen Lee's eyes moved to the sorrel. "I need a horse."

"Take the gun out of my face and we'll talk about it."

The woman hesitated, then shoved the revolver into the pocket of her skirt.

"When does the Fat Man plan to attack Green Meadow?" Drake asked. "Did I slow him some?"

"You didn't slow him any. What does the Fat Man care about a few dead men?"

"When does he attack?"

"Tomorrow, just before dawn."

"You're going to warn the town?"

"Drake, they won't listen to me. They'll think it's a story I made up to get them to sell cheap."

"There is no oil," Drake said.

"I know that. So does Rockefeller, so does everybody except the Fat Man."

Helen Lee's eyes locked on Drake's. "I can't save Green Meadow and neither can you. By this time tomorrow the town will be burning and everybody in it will be dead."

Drake frantically searched his mind for a solution. "I can tell the Fat Man that there's no oil."

"He'll call you a liar, Mr. Drake, then torture you to death. Besides, even if he did believe you it would make no difference. Tomorrow he'll rob the banks and loot the town. One way or another, the Fat Man always turns a profit."

"Then there's nothing we can do?" Drake said, defeat staring him in the face.

"Not a damn thing, Mr. Drake," Helen Lee said. "Now, do I get that horse?"

"You're running?"

"Yes, and I advise you to do the same thing."

"I reckon I'll stick."

"Then you'll die."

Chapter 41

Drake watched Helen Lee saddle the sorrel, making no offer to help. He'd told the woman he'd stick, and now he considered it the most stupid thing he'd ever said.

Stick why?

He couldn't save Green Meadow, and now he had Nancy to worry about. To stay here was to invite death, and he knew it.

Helen Lee was wasting no time saddling her horse and Drake figured she must reckon that Harvey Thornton and his gunmen were real close.

Drake was surprised when Nancy stepped into the barn. The girl was very pale, but he saw no tears.

"You are Helen Lee," Nancy said. She looked like she was in a trance—there, but far away.

Helen Lee swung into the saddle. "How did you know that? A lucky guess?"

"I don't guess. And you're not what you appear to be."

The women exchanged glances, a wordless, female communication that left Drake hopelessly trying to guess at its meaning.

"You have to leave here, girl," Helen Lee said. "This is a dangerous place."

"I know that also," Nancy said. "We will go with you."

"We have a burying to do," Drake said.

The girl turned and looked at him. "No, Chauncey. There's coal oil in the barn. Use it to set the cabin on fire. This is an evil, unhappy place, but Silas was a good man and his ashes will purify the ground."

"Is that how you want it?" Drake said. "It's rough, mighty raw."

"That's how Silas wants it," Nancy said.

"Get it done," Helen Lee said. "We don't have much time." She looked at Nancy again. "Who was Silas?"

"I'll tell you about him," Nancy said, "but not now. As you say, we don't have much time."

The cabin was ablaze as Drake and the two women rode away.

Nancy, riding Silas's rangy mule, said nothing, her eyes distant.

"I figure we should head south," Drake said to Helen Lee. "We can lose ourselves in the mountains."

"No, Mr. Drake, we're heading for Wilburton," the woman said.

Drake nodded. "As good a place as any, I guess. There's law in Wilburton."

Helen Lee turned to him. "Mr. Drake, John D. Rockefeller is there."

"I'm not catching your drift, lady."

"You will, Mr. Drake. Later, you'll understand everything."

Drake wondered at that. What was Helen Lee's connection to Rockefeller? And had she really fled the Fat Man, or was this all part of an elaborate plot hatched in the Fat Man's reptilian mind?

But what? His own death? That wasn't likely. Helen Lee could have shot him in the barn. A plan to assassinate Rockefeller? Again, not likely. Even the Fat Man wouldn't risk kicking over that hornet's nest. Killing a man as rich and powerful as Rockefeller was no small thing.

Drake gave it up. Helen Lee said he'd soon understand. He'd have to be patient until then.

As the night crowded close, they made their way through the pass west of Red Oak Peak, then headed due south to the wagon road.

The rutted trail was a moonlit ribbon aimed straight as an arrow westward and they would reach the town well before sunup. But after an hour, Helen Lee, tired as she was, insisted they take a break. They rode into a stand of hardwoods cut through by a stream to rest for thirty minutes.

Helen Lee took Nancy's head on her shoulder and gently stroked the girl's hair as she listened to her talk about Silas.

Again Drake wondered about the woman. Her display of tenderness toward Nancy was so out of character he couldn't come to grips with it.

Who was she? And what was she?

He could ask her, but would he get a straight answer? Probably not.

Drake decided to try a different tack.

"What's Wilburton town like, Miss Lee?" he said.

"Like nothing. It's not really a town and its only reason for existence is the railroad. Well, that and Robbers Cave close by. They say the James boys used to hide out in the cave in the old days. I don't know if it's true or not, but that's what they say."

Drake grinned, a passing thought pleasing him. "Is that where John D. Rockefeller is holed up? In a cave?"

"No. There's a hotel, if you can call it that. He and Karl Benz are there, or they were. Maybe they've gone back to Washington, I don't know."

"If Rockefeller knew there was no oil, why was he here?"

He was sure he knew the answer. He just wanted to hear the woman say it.

Helen Lee smiled. "Mr. Drake, curiosity killed the cat, you know."

"Yeah," Drake said, "it's a weakness of mine."

The woman gently pushed Nancy away from her. "Time to ride, honey," she said.

Drake shook his head. "Miss Lee, who the hell are you?"

"I'll tell you what I hope I am, Mr. Drake. I hope I'm the Fat Man's worst nightmare."

Chapter 42

It was still dark when Drake and the two women rode into quiet, dusty Wilburton, as yet untouched by this part of the Territory's coal boom.

At the end of the only street was a station platform and water tower, and catty-corner to its right a two-story adobe building with a corral out back.

"That's the hotel," Helen Lee said. "If John D. is still in town, he'll be there."

"We going to roust him out of bed?" Drake said.

"I don't advise it," the woman said. "He sleeps light and keeps a gun close."

Drake smiled. "Somehow I didn't figure him for a gun hand."

"You don't get to be a billionaire in this country without being tough, Mr. Drake, and Rockefeller is as tough as they come. Karl Benz is no pushover either."

"Neither are you, Miss Lee," Drake said.

The woman turned in the saddle and looked at him. "You can bet your sweet ass on that, Mr. Drake."

The darkness had stirred up a strong wind from the

south, blowing hard off the twelve-mile-long ridge of Blue Mountain.

Yellow sand drove across the street, and ahead of Drake a wooden bucket bounced and tumbled before it thudded into the wall of the hotel.

The wind roaring in his ears, Drake pointed to the corral and the two women swung their mounts in that direction, heads bent against the flaying sand.

They dismounted in the lee of the adobe where the horses were protected from the wind, then made their way to the front of the hotel.

The door was a heavy blanket that tossed in the wind. Drake pulled it aside and let the women enter, then followed them.

Inside was a single, windowless room with a few scattered tables and chairs. A bar opposite the door had a variety of bottles and jugs on its shelves. To the left of the bar a rickety staircase led to the rooms upstairs and on the far wall was an adobe stove with a cast-iron chimney.

A single oil lamp stood on the bar, its flame guttering in the breeze from the door, casting a dancing, orange light that moved the shadows.

There was no one in sight.

"I'm hungry," Nancy said, the first words she'd uttered since they'd left the shelter of the hardwoods. She looked tired as she rubbed her butt. The mule was not a comfortable animal to ride.

"I'll see if I can wake Juan," Helen Lee said.

She stepped to the bottom of the stairs and called out, loudly enough, "Juan! Can you come down?"

A minute passed, then another.

Finally Drake heard the thud of bare feet on the

steps and a small Mexican man appeared, his hair tousled. He wore a long white nightshirt and a sour expression.

"Who calls me in the middle of the night?" Juan said, peering around him.

"It's me, Juan. Helen Lee."

The Mexican's face cleared and he descended the last few steps at a run.

"Miss Lee, I never expected to see you again," he said, kissing the woman on the cheek.

Helen Lee smiled. "And it's good to see you again, Juan. Is Mr. Rockefeller here?"

"*Sí*, senorita. But he's very tired. He and Mr. Benz stayed up long last night, talking."

"We're hungry, Juan. Can you feed us?"

The little Mexican beamed. "When two beautiful senoritas brighten my poor house, of course I can feed you. Chicken stew, corn tortillas, and coffee. How does that sound?"

"Wonderful," Helen Lee said.

"Then take a seat, please. I'll bring the coffee soon."

The food was good and after they'd eaten, Drake built a cigarette and stepped to the door with his coffee.

He pulled the curtain aside and looked out. The wind was still whipping, lifting drifts of sand and dust from the street, and a ragged coyote trotted past, head down and miserable.

The night had grown a shade lighter, a harbinger of the dawn, and Drake felt a terrible sickness in him. Soon the town of Green Meadow would die, and by the time the sun rose to its highest point, it would be inhabited only by the dead.

Nancy stood by his elbow.

"You're thinking, Chauncey," she said.

Drake nodded. "Seems like."

"About Green Meadow?"

"Yeah. The people . . ."

"There was nothing you could do."

"I reckon. But it doesn't make it any easier."

"Come, sit down. Rest awhile."

Drake sat at the table again. He saw Helen Lee glance at his mutilated hand.

"How come you never asked me about it?" he said.

"I didn't need to. That's all Harvey Thornton and his boys talked about, how he shot off your fingers."

"And thumb."

Helen Lee nodded. "Thornton always does a thorough job."

"Is he doing it now, at Green Meadow?"

"Don't think about it, Mr. Drake. Nancy is right. There was nothing you could do, nothing any of us could do."

"I might have tried talking to Dub Halloran again."

Helen Lee managed a wisp of a smile. "He'd have tossed you in jail and thrown away the key."

"Well, I could have tried."

" 'I could have tried.' What am I hearing, Mr. Drake? Genuine guilt or self-pity?"

Drake accepted the barb. "A little of both, I guess."

"I suspect a little of one, and a lot of the other."

Nancy said, "And you, Helen, how do you feel?"

"It's a tragedy. But if the destruction of a town helps bring down the Fat Man, it's worth it in the end."

"That sounds cold," Nancy said.

"Does it? I didn't mean it to be. It's the cost of doing business."

"What business are you in, Helen?" Drake asked.

The woman turned and her glance moved to the top of the stairs.

"There is Mr. Rockefeller," she said. "Perhaps he'd like to tell you."

Chapter 43

"Miss Lee, I thought I heard your voice. Was it you that was doing all the hollering?"

"Sorry, J.D.," Helen Lee said. "I didn't mean to wake you."

"Well, you did, and poor Herr Benz is quite exhausted. German, you know."

Helen introduced Drake and Nancy. Drake saw Rockefeller glance at his mutilated hand, but as a man of breeding, the billionaire made no comment.

Rockefeller sat and Juan poured him coffee.

"What brings you here, Miss Lee?" Rockefeller said. Before the woman could reply, he said, "I have received no communication from the president, and I suspect he's washed his hands of the whole affair." The man's smile was wintry. "The Fat Man lives to fight another day."

Rockefeller lit his morning cigar and settled back in his chair. "That's a powerful wind outside," he said.

Drake studied the man. Rockefeller had the dusty, mummified look of the very rich, but his hazel eyes were lively and intelligent. His great dragoon mustache was neatly trimmed and his still hands showed no sign of ever having done manual labor.

"J.D., Mr. Drake has something to tell you," Helen said. "Events have turned out worse than we feared."

Rockefeller raised an eyebrow. "How could they get any worse? Mr. Drake?"

The door curtain flapped in the wind, allowing blowing sand and a flicker of thin daylight to enter.

"About now, the Fat Man is attacking the town of Green Meadow with fifty Texas gunmen," Drake said. "He plans to kill all the inhabitants, ransack the town, and set it on fire."

Drake hesitated a heartbeat, then said, "In other words, wipe it off the map."

Rockefeller ran a suddenly unsteady hand through his thin hair. "Ours was a harebrained scheme to begin with, but I never thought it would end like this."

"There's no oil," Drake said. "The town's dying for nothing."

The billionaire took a deep breath. "Mr. Drake, don't judge us too harshly. President Harrison's plan was to catch the Fat Man in the act of blackmailing the town. He thought the Fat Man would use the threat of violence to intimidate the people of the valley into selling their land cheap." He sighed. "To me."

"But then the murders began," Helen said. "We underestimated the man's viciousness."

Rockefeller said, "If President Harrison could, based on the testimony of myself, my colleague Herr Benz, and the Pinkertons, prove that the Fat Man was using blackmail and intimidation to cheat American citizens out of their land, he believed he could put the Fat Man away for several years as an enemy of the state. Of course, the wretch would never leave prison—the president would see to that."

"God help us, we encouraged the Fat Man to use his terror tactics," Helen said. "J.D. offered the settlers a ridiculously low price for their land, knowing they wouldn't sell. The plan was that when the Fat Man began to put pressure on the land and business owners, the army would intervene and arrest him."

Drake rolled a cigarette with one hand, a badge of honor among Texas cattlemen. He lit the cigarette and said, "I counted Reuben Withers as a friend."

"You speak of him in the past tense, Mr. Drake," Rockefeller said. "Where is he?"

"He's dead. He died trying to save my life."

Rockefeller looked like a man who had heard too much bad news all at once. "I'm sorry to hear that. He died bravely."

"He was a man," Drake said. "I think he died for nothing."

Helen brushed away a tear, but said nothing.

Finally, after a while, she said, "The Fat Man has too many friends in Washington, so the president asked the Pinkertons to assist him. Reuben was sent as a liaison between ourselves and his agency."

"And you, Miss Lee," Drake said. "What's your story?"

"What did Reuben tell you?"

Drake was angry at the world and he decided to be cruel.

"Helen Lee isn't your real name. You were born in Cork, Ireland, and later spent six months in jail in New Jersey for grand larceny. You're suspected of murdering two elderly men for their money. You run with a cheap tinhorn by the name of Henry Roberts, passing him off as your brother. In reality he's your common-law husband."

Drake sat back in his chair, smiling. "Did I miss anything important?"

"Not a thing, Mr. Drake," Rockefeller said. "Fortunately, none of it is true, except the part about Henry Roberts."

"Reuben and I made up a cover story that I could use if I was ever questioned by the Fat Man. As far as he was concerned, I'd be just another crook trying to buy land cheap."

"And Roberts?"

"He was part of my cover. Every time he touched me my skin crawled, but I needed him to prove my bona fides."

Helen smiled. "What was it old Queen Vic's mother told her on her wedding night? Just lie back, open your legs, close your eyes, and think of the empire. Well, when I was with Roberts, I thought of my country and finally being able to bring the Fat Man to justice."

"Miss Lee is my personal assistant," Rockefeller said. "She insisted she come with me, fearing that I couldn't fend for myself in the Wild West. In the event, that proved to be true."

He looked at Drake. "Like Reuben Withers, Miss Lee has made great personal sacrifices. She's a brave woman."

Juan sidled up to the table. "Breakfast, Mr. Rockefeller?"

"Can you boil an egg, my good man?"

"*Sí*. Very nice eggs."

"Two. Boil them for three minutes."

"*Sí*. Three minutes. Very good."

"Do you have any real bread instead of those horrible corn things?"

"*Sí*. Very good bread."

"Then bring me two eggs, bread, and butter."

"Very good, sir."

"Three minutes, mind."

"Yes. Very good. Three minutes."

Juan left, and Rockefeller's eyes moved to the door where the morning light was strengthening.

"It's all over," he said. "By now."

Nancy spoke for the first time, looking like a woman coming out of a trance. "Chauncey, I don't see it."

"See what?"

"The dying. Children aren't dying in Green Meadow."

Rockefeller, like many men of his class and time, had more than a passing interest in spiritualism. He looked at Nancy, his face betraying a quickening interest.

For her part, Helen Lee, being female, seemed to accept another woman's intuition without question.

"What do you see, dear?" she asked.

"Smoke . . . angry men . . . guns . . . death. But not the children. The children are not dying."

Slightly embarrassed, Drake said, "Nancy's ma was a Louisiana swamp witch. Sometimes she sees things."

"Did Green Meadow fight back?" Rockefeller said. "Did the Fat Man lose? Ask your spirit guide."

Drake's embarrassment turned to irritation.

"Let's stick to the facts, not . . . not ha'ants and stuff. When you or Miss Lee don't show up to share in the spoils, the Fat Man will know the game's over and head for Texas," Drake said to Rockefeller.

"Why Texas?" the man said.

"He has friends there, enough people to swear on a stack of Bibles that he never left the state."

"Then we must stop him before he gets there."

"Yeah, we must."

Rockefeller rose to his feet. "There's a telegraph at the station and I'll wire Washington. The president is going to get involved whether he wants to or not."

"Your eggs, senor," Juan said.

Rockefeller picked up an egg and a horn spoon and rapped the egg. Rapped harder.

"Damn it, man, how long did you boil these?" he said.

Juan beamed. "Ten minutes, like you said."

"They're as hard as rocks."

"No, no, Mr. Rockefeller. Ten minutes, very good."

"Ah, what the hell." Rockefeller stuck an egg in his pocket and began to peel the other. "I'm hungry enough to eat anything."

He stepped out the door into the dust storm, and headed for the station.

Chapter 44

An hour passed, then another, before Rockefeller returned.

His broadcloth suit was covered in dust and his eyes were red, smarting from hard-blown grit.

He sat at the table and lit a cigar before he spoke.

"I got the station master out of bed, then the president," he said. "Neither were real happy with me."

A silence stretched, and Drake's impatience grew. Finally he said, "What the hell happened?"

Rockefeller let smoke trickle between his thin lips. Then he said, "The president has ordered three companies of the Tenth Cavalry from Fort Sill to effect the capture of the Fat Man, dead or alive."

"When do they get here?" Drake asked, fearing the answer. Rockefeller did not disappoint him.

"One week hence, maybe longer."

Drake was stunned, and as far as he could tell, so was Helen Lee.

"Damn it, the Fat Man will be in Texas by then," he

said. "He'll have established his alibi and the cavalry won't be able to touch him."

"Mr. Drake, the military won't be hurried," Rockefeller said. "Apparently it takes time to prepare three companies of horse soldiers for the field."

Drake rose and stepped to the door. He pulled the curtain aside and without turning, said, "Then we go after him ourselves. Slow him down until the soldiers get here."

Rockefeller sounded alarmed. "We? Who exactly is we, Mr. Drake?"

"You, me, your friend Herr Benz, if he'll come."

"Mr. Drake, I'm a businessman," Rockefeller said. "Look at me. Do I look like a . . . a frontier tough to you?"

"No, you don't," Drake said. "But right now, you and Herr are all I've got."

"His name is Karl, Mr. Drake. Herr means *mister* in German."

"Herr, Karl, what's the difference? I need him and I need you. You were in the war, weren't you?"

"No, I hired a substitute. I would have made a terrible soldier."

"Out here a man doesn't hire a substitute to do his fighting."

Rockefeller rose to his feet, his face showing heat. "Mr. Drake, have you any idea what would happen to the stock exchange if I was killed? My death would plunge our great nation into a depression."

Now Drake felt the stab of his own anger. "Mr. Rockefeller, I don't give a damn about the stock exchange. You and the president cooked up some half-witted scheme to bring down an enemy of the state. Well, I could have gone along with that, but in the process you got a lot of innocent people killed. And that I can't forgive."

Drake stepped from the door to the table, invading Rockefeller's comfort zone. "Don't you think you owe those people something?"

"Yes, I do. And that's why I'm getting cavalry from Fort Sill."

"Too thin," Drake said. "You're carrying a rifle in my army, Mr. Rockefeller, and you're not hiring a substitute."

"And if I choose not to?"

"You said you aren't a frontier tough, but I am, and as bad and nasty as they come. You refuse to follow the colors, I'll shoot you down like a mangy yellow dog."

John D. Rockefeller was not used to being talked to that way, and he was momentarily struck dumb, his thin face pale with shock.

A harsh, irritable voice cut across the silence.

"Was ist das? Was redust du da?"

Karl Benz stood at the bottom of the stairs, a short, stocky man dressed in a high-button suit, celluloid collar, and striped tie, kid gloves on his hands.

Rockefeller recovered his composure, but was still shocked and angry. "For God's sake, Karl, speak English," he said. "Save that damnable German for your horse."

"John, I speak the language of Schiller and Goethe," Benz said with great dignity. "My horse does not."

He looked from the women to the white-lipped men standing almost nose to nose.

"I have intruded at a bad time, I think."

"It's not a bad time," Drake said. "I want you and Mr. Rockefeller to help me slow down the Fat Man's skedaddle into Texas."

"And you are?"

"Name's Chauncey Drake."

Benz clicked his heels and bowed. "And I am Karl Benz, genius, at your service." He looked at Drake. "Tell me about this . . . skedaddle."

After Drake had finished speaking, Benz bowed his head in thought.

After a while he nodded. "Ya, ya, ya, I understand. The Fat Man is an enemy of all mankind, not only Americans. He is a slave trader, the worst of them. He buys Chinese girls for a few dollars each and sells them to brothels all over the world."

Benz looked at the woman, then back to Drake. He lowered his voice to a whisper. "Do you know a Chinese girl's life expectancy in a brothel? Two to three years."

"Then you'll join me?"

"Ya, I will, Herr Drake." He drew himself up to his full, unimpressive height. "I see *mein* duty clear."

"Can you shoot?" Drake asked.

"Ya, I am a good shot. Once I had the great honor of hunting the Black Forest with His Royal Highness Crown Price Friedrich Wilhelm Nikolaus Karl. He told me I was a first-rate rifle."

Rockefeller shifted his feet. "You have shamed me, Karl. I turned Mr. Drake down, and now I feel guilty."

"John, *mein kamerad*, shame and guilt are noble emotions, essential for the maintenance of a civilized society. Both add to the development of some of the most refined qualities of human potential.

"But, all that aside, you can still step up and be a man."

Rockefeller held his silence for a long time.

Finally, his voice barely audible, he said, "Mr. Drake, I'm not a coward. But I just fought in one lost cause, and I've no appetite for another."

"This one we won't lose because we can't afford to," Drake said. "Will you saddle up and ride with me?"

"Yes. Yes, I suppose I will."

"A coward wouldn't do that," Drake said.

"*Nein, by Gott*, he wouldn't," Benz said, slapping Rockefeller on the back, rocking the billionaire's thin frame.

"Then why am I so scared?" Rockefeller said. He looked gaunt, dejected, dustier than usual.

"Because we all are." Drake looked at Benz and smiled. "Aren't we?"

The German grinned and whispered into Drake's ear, "I won't admit it in front of the *frauleins*, but ya, we are."

Chapter 45

"Mr. Rockefeller, you're the brains of this outfit," Drake said. "What will the Fat Man do?"

To Drake's surprise, the man looked directly at Nancy.

"What do you see, my dear?"

The girl shook her head. "Nothing."

"Then it's up to me," Rockefeller said. "The Fat Man had two options. He could have called his gunmen back to his hideout in the mountains to wait developments, or he immediately headed south for Texas."

"Ach, John, don't tell us what he could do, tell us what he did do," Benz said.

"I think he's in the mountains, but only if he did indeed destroy Green Meadow. Now he'll wait, expecting to hear from me or Miss Lee."

"He'd also want to know if the rest of the settlers are scared and pulling out," Drake said.

"And if he didn't destroy the town?" Helen said.

"Then he's lit a shuck for Texas," Drake said.

Drake took time to build and light a cigarette; then he said, "We'll head for Little Yancy Mountain and see if the Fat Man is there. If he's not, we'll ride south after him. His armored wagon cuts a clear trail."

He looked around the table. "Anybody got a better idea?"

Nobody had, and Drake nodded. "So be it. Let's saddle up and ride."

"I'll tell the station master what we intend," Rockefeller said. "Have him send the troops after us when they arrive."

"Nancy and I are coming with you, Mr. Drake," Helen said.

Drake smiled. "I didn't figure it any other way."

Away from Wilburton, the wind was no longer a stinging lash, but it shredded the trees on each side of the wagon road and slapped angrily against the five riders.

Drake thought he smelled rain, and to the south dark clouds were building above Blue Mountain.

He glanced behind him at his small command.

Rockefeller and Benz were well mounted on blood horses, Nancy on her mule taking up the rear with the packhorse. He turned to the front again, uncomfortably aware that he was asking two aging millionaires and a couple of women to slow the progress of one of the most ruthless criminals in history.

Benz was game, Rockefeller less so, but he'd stick. The women had the kind of quiet courage that endures and he had no doubts about either of them.

And of his own courage, Drake would not venture an opinion.

By the time they reached Red Oak Mountain the day tinted slate gray with the coming of evening and the keening wind had found an ally in the rain.

Drake led the way north through the pass, then crossed two miles of flat into the foothills of the Sans Bois.

Rockefeller and Benz had broken out slickers that they passed to the ladies, and by the time they reached the mountains, like Drake, they were well and truly soaked.

An arroyo thick with cedar and pine gave some shelter from the teeming downpour. They dismounted, and Nancy and Helen improvised a tent by spreading their slickers over lower branches and everyone huddled underneath.

But Drake swung into the saddle again.

"I'm going to check out the clearing," he said. He smiled at his companions, cowering and miserable under their meager shelter. "And no dancing or loud singing while I'm gone."

"Mr. Drake, you go to hell," Rockefeller said.

Drake laughed out loud. It seemed that even billionaires needed to vent now and then.

Drake rode through the wide valley that led to the cutoff toward Little Round Mountain. He swung due west, riding through heavily timbered country, then drew rein at the sound of hoofbeats behind him.

He pulled his Colt and swung the mustang around, only to thumb down the hammer as he saw Nancy astride her mule emerge from growing darkness and rain.

"Damn it, girl, I could have drilled you for sure," he said.

"You didn't really think I'd let you go alone, Chauncey?"

"Well, now you can head right back. I don't want a woman trailing along."

"I'm here and I'm staying," Nancy said, a stubborn frown wrinkling between her eyes. "Besides, it's getting too dark and there might be growly bears back there."

"And the Fat Man might be right ahead of us, girl. He's worse than any bear or boogerman."

"I'm coming with you, Chauncey Drake. There's no use in arguing the point."

Drake gave up. When a woman makes up her mind about something no amount of protesting is going to change it.

"All right, then," he said. "But stay close. And keep quiet."

"Yes, Chauncey," Nancy said in a stage whisper.

Drake shook his head, then led the way through the rain-lashed, hissing night.

He stepped out of the saddle at the mouth of the gully leading to the clearing and slid Silas's Henry out of the boot under Nancy's knee.

"Keep this ready until I get back," he said. "There could be a sentry posted on the rim."

"What if I see you come running?" the girl asked.

"Then shoot whatever is chasing me—man, bear, or boogerman."

Drake smiled and patted the girl's thigh, then clambered onto the top of the ridge.

Wary this time, he moved carefully, his Colt up and ready.

The trees stirred uneasily in the wind, sending down fat raindrops that bounced off Drake's hat. The ground was muddy underfoot, silencing the patches of gravel.

He reached the spot where his dynamite had done its damage.

Pines had been uprooted and a few huge boulders dislodged. It looked like a battle had been fought over this small patch of ground.

There was no sentry, he was sure of that.

After another twenty yards, the rim ended abruptly, a steep rock face falling away from where Drake stood to the flat.

But he could look out over the whole clearing from here, though most of it was shrouded in darkness.

There were no fires, and when he looked to the east he was sure the Fat Man's cabin was gone. Several tents still stood, inverted Vs of dull white in the gloom, but there was no sound and no movement from the camp, only the relentless racket of rain and wind.

Drake retraced his steps. Nancy emerged from under a tree, the Henry in her hands.

"Skedaddled," Drake said. "All of them."

He gathered the mustang's reins and walked forward, scouting the ground.

The soft earth was scarred by the tracks of heavy wheels.

Drake cursed under his breath.

The Fat Man was on his way to Texas.

Chapter 46

"The rain hasn't broken down the wheel tracks," Drake said.

"What does that mean?" Nancy said.

"It means the Fat Man's wagons passed this way not more than two, three hours ago."

"We just missed them, Chauncey."

"I reckon." Drake smiled. "Lucky for us."

He looked into the violent night. "I want to take a look at their camp."

"Why? They've gone."

"There might be something...I don't know... something..."

But Drake knew, he just didn't care to voice his forlorn hope aloud.

Maybe, by a miracle, Reuben Withers had survived and was now sheltering in one of the abandoned tents.

He was clutching at straws, he knew, but it was worth a few minutes of his time to find out for sure.

Nancy's face was pale under the brim of her battered hat.

"Only the dead, Chauncey," she said. "You'll find only the dead."

Drake nodded. "Maybe so, but let's do it."

Without another word, he led his horse forward . . . into yet another nightmare in a life that seemed full of them.

Drake stopped at the spot where the cabin had stood. Despite the rain, the dead-line was still visible and he was sure he could smell the man's vile stench.

Nancy felt the evil of the place. She recoiled in fear and quickly stepped away, the mule, head up and stiff-legged following her.

"Did you smell it?" Drake asked.

The girl nodded. "It's the stink of evil, Chauncey. Hell smells like that."

"Yeah, I guess it does. And I reckon it'll smell even worse once the Fat Man gets there."

Two blanket-wrapped bodies lay on the ground close to where the cabin stood. Both had been hit by gun-shots and died hard from belly wounds.

"What's that?" Nancy said. "Over there in the trees."

Drake's eyes followed her pointing finger. A shimmering white gleam was visible through the rain, like an alabaster column in the darkness.

"I don't know what it is," Drake said. "But I got the feeling it's gonna turn out to be nothing good."

He led the mustang toward the trees, Nancy following him.

Despite being nailed to a huge hickory and disemboweled, the pain-distorted face of the man was still recognizable.

It had taken Henry Roberts a long time to die, and

even a tinhorn like he was had not deserved that kind of death.

"Poor man," Nancy said. "What an awful way to die."

"Helen Lee ran out on the Fat Man, so he took his revenge on good ol' Henry."

"Chauncey, can you get him down?"

Drake shook his head. "He's nailed up there pretty good. The coyotes will bring him down."

"That's a terrible thing to say."

"Nancy, he brought it on himself. Isn't my fault, isn't your fault, and we owe him nothing."

"He was a human being."

"So was Reuben Withers," Drake said. He held up his stump of a hand. "And me."

He let his words hang in the air, then looked around him at the desolate camp. "Let's get back and join the others."

But the Fat Man's lingering, malevolent presence was not done with Chauncey Drake quite yet.

"Help me . . ."

The voice was thin, weak, and it came from inside one of the tents.

"Who's there?" Drake said.

"Here. Over here. In the tent."

Drake's gun sprang into his hand. "Nancy, stay here," he said.

The girl raised her rifle. "Got you covered, Chauncey."

Stepping cautiously, Drake walked to the tent, then stopped. "Who's inside?" he said.

"Just me, Will Convey . . . out of"—the man was having trouble speaking—"out of Red River county, Texas."

"Do you have a gun?"

"No gun. I'm done with that. Threw my Colt gun away."

Drake opened the tent flap and stepped inside.

"Kept my rifle, though," the man on the cot said, as though he was unaware that Drake was there. "Pa an' me will need it fer deer huntin' come fall."

Drake lifted the man's blanket. His belly and lower chest were covered in dried blood, death wounds that kill a man slow.

"How old are you, son?" Drake asked.

"Just gone eighteen."

"What happened to you?"

"Town. Damned, accursed town." The kid's eyes were dimming, frantically trying to focus on Drake. "They was waiting for us, mister. Them damn pumpkin rollers had scouts out like sod'jers, seen us coming from a fur piece off."

"Green Meadow? Was that the town?"

"They'd laid fer us. Cut us down in the street like dogs. Seen Brad Collins get it an' Sam'l Price. Lee Fours got his head smashed in with a sledgehammer an' his brains went everywhere."

The kid grimaced, fighting pain. "Damned farmers an' storekeepers were waiting fer us. We scattered an' they went after us, shooting us down, hangin' some. Seen that, a man gettin' hung."

"Green Meadow?"

"Yeah, that's what they called the place. I call it hell-fire."

"Will, where is Harvey Thornton and the Fat Man?"

"Gone. Back to Texas. They wouldn't take me with them, said I was going to die soon anyhow."

"How many with them?"

"Are you the law, mister?"

"No, I'm not the law. How many with the Fat Man?"

"Thornton, maybe six more. That's all that's left. Damned sodbusters killed 'em all."

The kid saw Nancy step inside and smiled. "Sorry I can't rise, purty lady," he said. "My ma teached me manners and my ciphers. She'd take a switch to me if'n she knew I didn't rise when a lady entered."

"You just lie still," Nancy said. She pushed hair off the boy's fevered forehead. "You'll be just fine."

"Ma'am, go to Red River county, Texas. Ask anybody where the Convey ranch is an' they'll point her out. Tell Ma I'll see her in the fall. Tell her I don't ride with Teeter McCallum an' that wild bunch no more. Just . . . just tell her I'm coming home."

"You're going home to Texas by another road, boy," Drake said. "Take your medicine and make your peace with God. Your time is short."

Nancy gave Drake a disapproving, sidelong look, but Drake said, "The boy's old enough to carry a gun, he's old enough to know the truth."

He looked at Convey. "We got to be moving on, boy."

"No, stay with me." His eyes tried to find Nancy. "Take my hand, ma'am," he said. "I'm so almighty sceered of dying."

Nancy held the kid's hand; then she watched all the light go out of him.

She was quiet for a long time, then said, "So much dying, Chauncey. When will it end?"

"Soon," Drake said, "when I put a bullet into the Fat Man."

Nancy was again silent, and when she finally spoke

her voice was hollow, distant. "The Fat Man can't be killed, not by any mortal man."

Despite himself, Drake felt a chill.

"Then what can kill him, for God's sake?"

"A dead woman, Chauncey. Only a dead woman can kill him."

Chapter 47

When Drake returned to the arroyo he was pleased that Benz greeted him with a raised rifle. The German was born ready and he had bark on him.

In reply to a barrage of questions, Drake told them about the abandoned camp and the last words of the dying kid.

"The Fat Man took a beating at Green Meadow," he said. "The town didn't die as easily as he figured it would."

"Ha, there were *soldaten* there, perhaps," Benz said. He read the question on Drake's face and said, "Soldiers."

"Old soldiers," Drake said, the rain falling around him like steel needles. "During the war, Sy Goldberg led an infantry regiment at twenty, a brigade at twenty-one. Jim Lands, the blacksmith, fit Apaches and before that Comanche. And there are dozens of others just like them in Green Meadow. Men like those are no bargain."

"But who could have warned them?" Rockefeller said.

"I don't know. But whoever he is, he's a friend."

"What do we do now?" Helen Lee asked.

"We'll go after him at first light," Drake said. "The armored wagon will slow them down, and we'll slow them even more."

Drake dismounted, then led the horses into the shelter of the trees.

When he rejoined Nancy and the others, he squatted under the dripping roof of the slickers, suddenly weary.

"I could sure use coffee about now," he said to no one in particular.

Rockefeller rose, fumbled in his saddlebags, and came up with a pint bottle. "It's not coffee," he said, "but will this whiskey do?"

"Close enough," Drake said, grinning.

Sometime in the night, as the others lay in restless sleep, Nancy undid the bandages on Drake's hand, then sniffed each stump.

"No rot, Chauncey," she whispered. "And there's some healing."

"Still hurts like hell," Drake said.

"It will and for a long time to come."

The girl bound up Drake's hand again, then laid her head on his shoulder.

The coyotes yipped close and the trees ticked raindrops, but Nancy did not hear. Within moments she was asleep, her head growing heavy.

Bone tired, Drake stared into the darkness. Lightning scrawled across the big-bellied clouds above Little Yancy Mountain and thunder rumbled like the drums of advancing barbarians.

Drake did not fear the thunder; he feared the morning and what it would bring. Life for some, death for others, and all of it would be of his own choosing.

He lifted his face, closed his eyes, and let errant raindrops cascade over his cheek and forehead. The water was cool, clean, a baptism of sorts for a man born to misfortune.

The dawn brought no end to the rain.

Riding through a downpour, Drake cut the Fat Man's trail just north of heavily wooded Fourche Maline Creek and beckoned the others forward.

A couple of cottonwoods on the opposite bank showed fresh rope scars on their trunks, suggesting that the armored wagon had run into difficulty during the crossing.

Drake smiled, something red and fierce inside him. The Fat Man was not making good time.

After scouting the area for thirty minutes, Drake picked up the wagon tracks again, heading east. The wheel ruts were still fresh, so the Fat Man and his gunmen were not far ahead.

After half a mile the tracks swung due south again, into a natural cut in Limestone Ridge. This was wooded, rolling country, but presented no real obstacle to the passage of wagons.

Drake drew rein and waited on the others. They sat their mounts in lashing rain and held a council of war.

Rockefeller, looking wet and miserable, glanced along their back trail. "The horse soldiers will never find us in this wilderness," he said.

"They'll have Indian scouts out, maybe Apache," Drake said. "I reckon they'll find us all right if they have a mind to."

"Well, Mr. Drake," Helen said. "You're the general. Where do we go from here?"

"I've been studying on it," Drake said. "Benz says he's good with a rifle—"

"I am," the German said.

"So Karl and me will ride on ahead, cut in front of the Fat Man, and then lay a world of hurt on him."

"And the rest of us?" Rockefeller said.

"Will follow his trail, but don't get too close."

"Suppose you two don't come back?" Helen asked. Her eyes were cool.

"Then hightail it out of here and find those pony soldiers."

Drake turned to Benz. "Karl, we'll head into the hills and ride south, keeping just to the west of the Fat Man. It's broken country and rough going."

"I'm an excellent rider, Herr Drake," Benz said. "But then, I'm excellent at most things."

Drake nodded. "Let's just hope you're as good with a rifle as you say you are. This is not a sure thing and dangerous."

"No, it's not a sure thing," Nancy said, looking at Drake. "Not a sure thing at all."

Chapter 48

Drake and Benz rode into rugged hill country, isolated stands of pine and wild oak in the hollows. The day was wild with rain and wind, battering at Drake and Benz, full of spite. Clouds hung so low a man on a horse could reach out and touch them and grab a fistful of mist that would vanish in his hand like a fairy gift.

After a mile they rode up on a narrow valley, cut across by a fast-moving creek. On a hunch, Drake swung west, following the bank.

After a couple hundred yards, the creek meandered south, taking the line of least resistance around a gradual rise crested by scrub and oak.

Drake stepped out of the saddle and indicated to Benz that he should do the same thing.

Talking over wind and rain, Drake said they would go on foot to the top of the rise. "I'm betting the wagons got stuck in the creek," he yelled.

Benz, stocky, Teutonic and durable, nodded, then slid a Winchester out of the saddle boot.

"You ready?" Drake asked.

"Ready, *mein* general."

"I'll point out the targets and you'll do the business with the rifle." Drake brought his face close to the German's. "Don't miss."

"Karl Benz does not miss."

"But no bang-bang until I tell you. Understand?"

"Mr. Drake," Benz said with great dignity, "I'm not a child."

"Good. Then let's get it done."

Despite rain and mud underfoot, the climb to the top of the rise was not difficult.

Drake and Benz lay down in the brush and crawled the last couple of yards on their bellies.

Drake had expected to see the armored wagon still in the creek, but it was now safe on the other side, the ox team head down, taking a breather.

Harvey Thornton was mounted, talking at a grilled window to someone inside the armored wagon.

Drake would have dearly loved to take a pot at him, but the plan was to slow the Fat Man's progress, not kill his gunmen. At least not yet.

He nudged Benz and brought his mouth close to the man's hairy ear.

"Shoot the two lead oxen, Karl," he said. "The cows, you understand?"

The German nodded. He nestled the butt of the Winchester against his left shoulder.

Drake felt a pang of doubt. He had never met a wrong-handed rifleman who could shoot worth a damn.

But he had no time to ponder the question, because Benz's rifle roared and the lead ox went down in a tangle of harness and kicking legs.

Benz fired again. A second ox went down.

For a moment or two, Thornton and his remaining gunmen seemed paralyzed, surprised by the sudden attack.

But now Thornton had his rifle out, shooting into the smoke drift at the top of the rise.

Drake took a pot at the gunman with his Colt. Missed. Tried again. Missed a second time.

Now all six of the Fat Man's remaining men were shooting and bullets clipped the branches of the oaks around Drake and Benz.

Drake swore. It was time to light a shuck.

He bellied backward, Benz doing the same, then rose and sprinted down the hill toward the horses.

Drake was in the saddle by the time Thornton and the others topped the rise. Bullets kicked up V's of mud around him and one came close enough to tug at the sleeve of his shirt.

Benz, his fighting blood up, was yelling German cuss words that Drake thought sounded a sight better than American ones.

"Get out of here, Karl!" he yelled.

Benz swung into the saddle, then cried out as he was hit.

Drake triggered a couple of shots in the direction of Thornton, then grabbed the reins of Benz's horse.

He headed back down the creek bank at a gallop, Benz clinging to the saddle horn, his bearded face white with shock.

Glancing back, Drake saw no sign of pursuit. He reckoned Thornton had few enough men without risking more in a running gunfight.

But there's always someone who doesn't get the message.

A rider broke away from the group on the rise, ignored Thornton's yells to stop, and hit the flat at a fast gallop, a Colt held muzzle up in his right hand, cavalry style.

Suddenly all Drake's pent-up rage against the Fat Man and Thornton rose in him like coffee bubbling over in a pot. His vision narrowed to a back-rimmed tunnel, at its center a lanky Texan coming at him, game and full of fight on a buckskin horse.

He swung the mustang around and shucked his Colt. By his count, he'd only one round left and there was no time to reload. It would have to be enough.

The two riders closed fast. Under his mustache, the Texan's lips were peeled back from his teeth.

Fifty yards . . . forty . . . thirty . . .

The Texan fired.

A clean miss.

Twenty yards . . .

Another shot from the gunman, a second miss.

Ten yards . . .

Both men fired at the same time.

Drake aimed for the Texan's chest. He felt the mustang shudder, then the grass, and sky cartwheeled toward him. He hit the ground hard, rolled and screamed in pain as his mutilated hand was crushed by the buckle of his gun belt.

Aware of the terrible danger he was in, Drake staggered to his feet. Thornton and another man were riding toward him, guns blazing. He hit the ground again.

Another gun firing, the flat statement of a rifle.

Drake lifted his head. Thornton and the man with him had turned and were galloping back toward the rise. Bullets followed them, splitting the air around them.

He turned, expecting to see Benz shooting. But the man was slumped over in the saddle a distance away, allowing his horse to carry him out of the fight.

There was no time to puzzle over the rifleman. Drake rose to his feet and looked around him. His mustang lay sprawled on the ground, its neck broken, a bloody bullet wound in its chest. The Texan he had fought was still in the saddle, but hit hard, coughing up black blood.

Drake found his gun, stepped to the dying Texan, and dragged him out of the saddle, letting his body thud onto the ground. The man groaned, but did not speak.

The buckskin stood while Drake mounted. His left hand was on fire and he favored it, holding it against his chest. He kicked the buckskin into motion and trotted after Benz.

Riding toward them through the rain, his rifle butt on his thigh, was the skinny figure of John D. Rockefeller, grinning.

When he was close enough, the man said, "I guess I arrived in the nick of time, Mr. Drake."

"You surely did," Drake said.

"Karl Benz is not the only one who can shoot, you know," Rockefeller said.

He sounded more than a little miffed.

Chapter 49

A bullet had grazed the top of Benz's left shoulder, ranged downward, and probably chipped his collarbone. The wound didn't look serious to Drake, but the German would do no more shooting off his left shoulder for a while.

"I'm sorry, Herr Drake," Benz said. "Just into the fight, then out of it again."

"You did your part, Karl," Drake said. "Stood to your work like a man."

"We found a limestone cave in the hills," Rockefeller said. "We'll take him there."

"I told you and the others to follow the Fat Man's trail at a safe distance," Drake said, "not go traipsing through the hills."

"I know, but I don't take orders worth a damn," Rockefeller said. "And the women are even more insubordinate than I am."

The cave was a fracture in a limestone outcropping that had dissolved over centuries down to bedrock and formed a hollow twelve feet wide, eight feet high, and twice that deep.

At a distance, pines and wild oak concealed the entrance so well that Drake was almost on top of the cave before he realized it was there.

Drake helped Benz into the cave while Rockefeller led the horses to a stand of trees where they'd be out of the worst of the rain.

To Drake's joy, the women had coffee smoking on the fire and he helped himself to a cup as Nancy examined the German's shoulder.

After a while she said, "Your collarbone is broken, Mr. Benz."

The man nodded. "Ach, I thought as much." He looked at Drake. "No more bang-bang. And I can't use a . . . pistol."

Drake smiled at him. "As I told you before, you've already done your part."

But the steady German was a serious loss, fifty percent of his fighting force, if he discounted the women. Helen Lee could shoot and she'd do in a pinch. Girls like Nancy grew up around guns, and she too could be pressed into service if the need arose.

When Rockefeller returned, a tall, hollow-eyed man dripping rain, Drake recounted the attack on the Fat Man and his encounter with the charging Texan.

"Lost my mustang," he said. "He was a good hoss."

"I'd say the buckskin is fair exchange," Rockefeller said.

"Maybe so, but I liked that mustang. He was mean and ugly, but he was steady."

"Like poor Karl." Helen smiled.

"Yeah, just like poor Karl."

Drake drained his coffee, then rose to his feet.

"Anybody got a knife?" he said.

Rockefeller reached into his pocket and produced an English folding knife. "Will this do?"

"Perfect," Drake said. "And I want to borrow a slicker."

"What are you doing, Herr Drake?" Benz asked, then winced as Nancy slid his arm into a sling she'd made from the sleeve of the German's shirt.

"We need another rifleman," Drake said. "And I reckon that's me."

He looked into the racketing rain and arrowheads of pine that looked black in a day as gray as flint.

"Come dark, I plan to pay the Fat Man another visit."

"Chauncey, do you think that's wise?" Nancy said. "He'll be waiting for you."

"I don't think he will. I reckon it's the last thing he'll expect, that we didn't just hit and run."

"What will you do?" Rockefeller asked.

"Stir him up a tad. The Fat Man took a beating at Green Meadow, and his confidence is shaken. I want to remind him that he's in a war, and keep on reminding him."

Drake shrugged into the slicker and stood at the cave entrance, looking at Benz.

"Karl, you're going back."

"But, *mein herr*—"

"You can't shoot and if you stay all you'll do is get in the way. You'd be a useless mouth to feed."

Helen Lee looked at Drake with loveless eyes. "I thought you said he'd done his part."

"He did, and he can help us again. Karl, find those

pony soldiers and tell them where we are, or were. If you have to, guide them yourself."

Drake expected an argument, but Benz was a realist, and his bleak gaze told Drake that he fully understood the situation. He said, "I will find the *soldaten*. I will bring them."

"Thank you," Drake said. "You're true blue."

Drake stepped out of the cave, then turned. "And one more thing, Karl. Leave your rifle when you go."

It took Drake thirty minutes to find the Y-shaped branch he needed, and another thirty to cut it from the tree with the puny folding knife.

He stripped off bark and leaves, then hacked the arms of the Y down to six inches, holding the branch between his knees. The lower limb he cut to twelve and sharpened into a point.

Drake admired his handiwork at arm's length and smiled. It would make a dandy rifle rest. But whether or not it would make him a better marksman remained to be seen.

When he returned to the cave, Benz was already gone.

Maybe it was Helen Lee's long association with wealthy business tycoons that made her decide, out of some kind of loyalty, not to let it go.

"You hurt him, Drake," she said. "Hurt him real bad."

"He'll get over it," Drake said.

"If he can survive out there with a broken shoulder and no gun."

"My dear, I'm sure Karl will manage," Rockefeller said. "He's a tough little man. German, you know, and all that."

"But Mr. Drake more or less threw him out," Helen said.

Drake smiled. "Not more or less, Miss Lee. I really did throw him out. My concern is to keep you and Nancy and Mr. Rockefeller alive, and myself. We don't have room for passengers on this trip."

"It was shabby, heartless, and underhanded," Helen said.

"Describes me perfectly, don't it?" Drake grinned.

Chapter 50

"Let me go with you, Mr. Drake," Rockefeller said.

"Not this time, Mr. Rock— Wait, can I call you John? Mr. Rockefeller is a mouthful."

"Of course you can. We're friends, after all."

"Call me Chauncey."

"Yes . . . an unfortunate name to be sure, but all right, it's Chauncey."

"I need you here at the cave, John," Drake said. "We need to be prepared for anything. The Fat Man could have stray gunmen in these hills."

"I understand. I'll make sure the ladies are safe."

Drake stepped into the saddle and shoved the forked stick into the scabbard with Benz's rifle.

"Rain isn't ever going to let up, is it?" Rockefeller said. He handed Drake a slicker.

Drake glanced at the black sky. "Seems like."

"Nancy is worried about you, Chauncey."

"I know she is, and I worry about her. That's the reason I want you to stay here."

"I'll take care of her. She's a nice girl and she has the

gift of second sight, but until now her life has been hard."

"Maybe a lot harder than either of us can imagine. Maybe harder than she'll ever want to tell." Drake touched his hat. "I'm riding."

"Good luck, Chauncey."

"Thanks. Same to you."

Drake swung the buckskin into the storm, lightning flashing above him. Thunder boomed close, and the pines took notice, trembling in the wind like virgins on their wedding night.

Drake again followed the creek east. Swollen with rain, cascades of white water showed here and there and formed dark whirlpools in the eddies.

The buckskin was a steady mount, seemed eager for the trail and showed no fear of thunder.

When the rise came in sight, Drake swung out of the saddle and let the reins drop. He slid the stick and the Winchester from the boot, then stopped in his tracks as he spotted movement out the corner of his eye, off to his right.

The dead Texan still lay sprawled on the ground, the wind tugging at his red bandana, waving it like a flag.

Drake stepped over to the man.

The Texan looked older than he remembered, hard in the face. His belt gun had been taken, and the little finger of his left hand had been cut off, probably to remove a ring.

A grim smile touched Drake's lips. It seemed that Thornton was determined to leave every man in the territory, alive or dead, missing fingers.

He felt nothing for the dead man. The Texan had

taken his chances, the odds at evens, but had tossed losing dice. It happened that way sometimes.

Better him than me, Drake decided.

He looked at the dead man one last time, shook his head, then turned his steps toward the rise, walking in rain.

The arrogance of Harvey Thornton stunned Drake.

Despite a bloody defeat at Green Meadow and a sneak attack that killed one of his men, the gunman had a large fire going, the flames protected by a rock overhang.

Two men squatted by the fire, watching a coffeepot on the coals, but as far as Drake could tell neither was Thornton. That left the gunman and two of his men unaccounted for.

Drake was uneasy. Where the hell was Thornton?

The two dead oxen still lay on the ground, but the armored wagon had been pulled closer to the trees, scarlet firelight reflecting on its front and side.

As far as Drake could tell, the horse line was behind the wagon where the animals would be protected from gunfire.

Drake spiked the rifle rest into the soft ground, then settled his rifle in the V. He figured after his first shot, he might be able to work the rifle and get off another. But, for a one-handed shooter, nothing was a certainty.

One thing he did know—he would have to kill a man.

A shot into the simmering coffeepot would be spectacular and cause all kinds of calamity, but would do nothing to cut down the odds and leave the Fat Man stranded.

Drake moved the Winchester and laid the sights squarely on the broad back of the man to the right of the fire.

He took a deep breath, let some of it out, took up the slack, and stroked the trigger as gently as a man caressing his mistress.

Blam!

The man by the fire stood, clawing for his gun.

Drake cursed.

Damn it, I missed him.

He rolled on his back, left forearm holding the rifle in place while he worked the lever. Rain battered on his face and ran into his mouth.

Bullets chipped through the trees above Drake's head. A man shooting uphill will usually hold too high and the gunmen down below were no exception.

Drake got back onto his belly and took in the scene at a glance.

He hadn't missed. The man he'd shot was facedown in the fire, coffee from the upturned pot throwing up steam by his head.

The other man had taken cover behind a wagon wheel, and Drake heard the Fat Man shriek inside, demanding to know what was happening.

Drake took a fast pot at the man by the wheel, then backed down the rise. The buckskin had not stood like the mustang, but had wandered a ways into the trees.

Cursing the animal, Drake grabbed the reins and climbed into the saddle. He kicked the horse into a gallop, crashed through the pines, then charged headlong into the rain-spun darkness.

Chapter 51

Drake almost missed the cave.

There was no fire to guide him, no female voices carrying like bells in the wind.

Signs of a struggle were everywhere.

Blood had splashed on a rock inside the cave, a single .44-40 shell casing lay on the sand and the coffeepot had been overturned.

Of the two women and Rockefeller there was no trace. Karl Benz had gotten away earlier, probably clean, but Drake had no way of knowing if that was the case.

Drake thumbed a match into flame and studied the cave floor. As he'd expected, two men wearing high-heeled boots had left tracks.

No doubt one of them had been Harvey Thornton.

By nature, Chauncey Drake was a brooding man, but he refused to sit and stew over the consequences of what had happened.

Action would decide how it all turned out in the end, not worry. A man's troubles were like people: They grew bigger if you nursed them.

Drake coaxed the fire's last few coals back into life and threw on more of the wood the women had gathered.

He refused to think about Nancy. Fretting over her would weaken him.

He took the coffeepot and stepped out of the cave into the rain. Water streamed down the rock shelf at several points and he had no difficulty filling it.

Half a sack of Arbuckle was still in the cave, ignored by Thornton. Drake tossed a handful into the pot and moved it onto the coals.

By the time he'd taken care of the buckskin, the coffee was on the boil, its fragrance filling the cave.

The rain was still falling, but the wind had grown even stronger, screaming like a banshee among the trees, gusting enough to spiral the flames of the fire.

Drake smoked and drank coffee, listening into the howling night. He did not expect Thornton to come back, but he kept his Colt close to hand.

He threw more wood onto the fire, stretched out on the sand, and slept.

At one point in the night a dog coyote trotted to within yards of the cave, then stopped, its muzzle lifted, reading the wind. After a few moments, it turned and ran down the rise, yipping.

Drake slumbered on . . .

At three in the morning, the wind shifted, coming from the north, but it held no memory of winter and blew warm, full of bluster, content to rock the pines and shred the wildflowers.

Drake did not waken . . .

Finally the dawn lit up the inside of the cave and Drake woke.

And all his problems woke with him.

The rain had stopped and a growing patch of blue sky elbowed the clouds aside. But the wind was blowing hard, rippling the grama grass.

Drake glanced inside the coffeepot, then laid it on the fire.

He built a cigarette and smoked, waiting for the pot to boil.

"Hey, you in the cave!"

It was Thornton's voice.

Drake stood and leaned out into the wind.

"Thornton, you son of a bitch, what do you want?"

"You know me, Chauncey. You know what I can do."

"I know you fer a cheap, two-bit tinhorn and yellow-bellied coward."

"Come out and see me, Chauncey. I won't shoot, but you'll look at what I've got with me and be mighty afeared."

"Is it Nancy? Thornton, if you hurt her, I'll—"

"Come and see, Chauncey."

Gun in hand, Drake stepped out of the cave and walked to the top of the rise, keeping to the cover of the trees.

Two men stood at the bottom of the hill, Thornton and one other. Thornton's arm was around Nancy's upper chest and he held a wicked-looking bowie knife to her throat. The second man stood by, alert and ready with a rifle.

"Do you know this woman, Chauncey?" Thornton said, grinning, his strange, tattooed eye fixed, unblinking.

"Yes, damn you, I know her."

The gunman pressed on the knife and a thin ribbon of blood appeared on Nancy's white throat.

"You won't know her once she's been skun, Chauncey," Thornton said. "And them others with her. I've never skun a billionaire afore, but there's a first time for everything, ain't there, Chauncey?"

Drake thought about making a play, but immediately dismissed the idea. Shooting at Thornton without harming Nancy was well-nigh impossible.

"What do you want, Thornton?" he asked.

"Just this—you lay off, Chauncey, y'hear? Oncet we're back in Texas, I'll let the women and that Rockefeller ranny go."

Drake didn't answer right away, and Thornton said, "Be afeared of me, Chauncey. I've skun a woman afore and I'm ready to do it again."

"Don't listen to him, Chauncey," Nancy yelled. "He'll kill us all anyway."

Using the back of his fist, Thornton hit Nancy hard on the side of her head. The girl fell at his feet.

Instinctively, Drake went for his gun.

The rifleman with Thornton brought his rifle up, but the big gunman stepped in front of him.

"Is that how you want to play it, Chauncey?" he said.

He dragged Nancy to her feet by her hair, and pressed the knife into her belly. "Do I start skinnin', Chauncey?"

"Leave her be, Thornton," Drake said. He holstered his Colt. "Let Nancy go and I'll step aside. You can take the Fat Man to Texas."

Thornton laughed. "You any idea how he's stinking up that wagon? Sooner we get him there, the better."

"I won't try to stop you. Now leave Nancy here."

"That's thin, Chauncey, way too thin. Like I told you, we'll drop her off somewhere in Texas."

Thornton was quiet for a moment, then said, "An' Chauncey, I see you come anywhere near her, and she dies. You know how long it takes a skun woman to die?"

Drake knew he was beaten. "I won't come near."

"Damn right you won't." Thornton grinned.

He waved the other man away. Dragging Nancy with them, they mounted their horses and left at a trot, the gunmen laughing at something Thornton had just said.

Drake felt like he'd just been kicked in the gut. He doubled over and dropped to his knees, groaning, felled by the terrible sense of loss that comes only when a man loses someone he loves more than himself.

Chapter 52

The return of the rain drove Chauncey Drake back to the cave.

He sat beside the untended fire, head down, knees drawn up to his chest, the stump of his maimed hand against his body.

He felt like a beaten dog, hurting all over, the worst of it inside him.

How long Drake would have stayed that way was something he could never determine because a man's voice roused him to a present reality.

"Hello, the camp!"

Drake rose to his feet and stumbled to the mouth of the cave.

"Damn you, Thornton, you checking on me?"

"Recognize you by that whining voice, son. But this ain't Thornton, Wayfarer. This here is Deputy Marshal Washita Jolly out of Judge Isaac Parker's court."

A pause, then he said, "You owe me seventy-nine dollars an' fifty cents, remember?"

"Yeah, well, I don't have it, and the damned horse you sold me is dead."

"Figured you fer a piker, Wayfarer. Anyhoo, I'm coming in, and don't let me see no gun in your hand. Your good hand, that is."

Jolly rode up to the cave, a big, cold-eyed man on a tall bay, with the former outlaw's habit of never letting his gaze rest on any one place for too long.

He drew rein and studied Drake. "Hell, boy, you look even worse than the last time I seen you. Real peaked, like."

"You come all this way for seventy-nine dollars, Marshal?"

"Nope, though it is a considerable amount of money. I ran ol' Luke an' the Apache all the way to Fort Smith, then headed back south on the Katy Flyer. At the judge's expense, let me add."

"How come?"

"Wayfarer, you gonna invite me in fer a cup of coffee, us being near friends an' all?"

"You're not my friend, and the name's Drake."

"Suit yourself, Wayfarer."

"Step down." Drake sighed. "I'll boil up some coffee."

Drake watched Jolly light a slim black cheroot with a brand from the fire, then said, "How did you find me?"

"I almost didn't. I backtracked to the last place I'd seen you and scouted around for a spell, but there was neither hide nor hair. Finally figured on heading for that town you mentioned, what's it called?"

"Green Meadow."

"Yeah, that's the place. But then I got lucky. Met a

ranny on the trail, a furriner with a shot-up shoulder, and he told me where you might be."

"His name is Karl Benz and—"

"And he's out looking for three companies of the Tenth Cavalry that's maybe lost an' scared. Yeah, I know. He told me."

"What else did he tell you, Marshal?"

"About the Fat Man getting whupped at Green—whatever the hell it is—and heading for Texas."

"Did Karl tell you why Green Meadow was attacked, that Washington fouled the whole thing up?"

"What whole thing?"

"The president's plan to catch the Fat Man in the act of terrorizing a town and bring him to justice."

Jolly grinned, yellow horse teeth clamped on his cigar. "Nobody in Washington is worth a hill of beans, including the president."

"How come you decided to believe me, Marshal?"

"Hell, boy, I didn't, not at first. But then I got to thinking, 'Washita, what if that crazy wayfarer's big windy is true?' Well, like I told you, I run ol' Luke an' the Indian all the way to Fort Smith an' spoke to the judge." Jolly held out his cup. "Fill that, boy."

"Damn it, what did Judge Parker say?" Drake asked, pouring coffee into Jolly's cup.

"He's heard of the Fat Man, said he was the . . . what the hell did he say? Oh, yeah, I remember, said he was 'an international criminal of the worst sort, a man who should have been hanged years ago.' Then he told me to put my foot on the Katy Flyer, then try and find you. Failing that, I was to enlist the help of the nearest city lawmen to assist me in the apprehension of the Fat Man."

Jolly spat into the fire. "City lawmen, my ass. Bunch of whore-humpin' pansies."

"You haven't heard the half of it, Marshal," Drake said.

He told Jolly about Nancy and how she, Helen Lee, and Rockefeller were now in the Fat Man's hands.

"If I go anywhere near their wagons, Harvey Thornton will kill Nancy," Drake said. "He said he'd skin her alive."

Jolly nodded. "And he will. Me an' Harv go back a long ways, and when he says he'll do a thing, he generally means it."

"Have you tried to arrest him before?" Drake asked.

"Hell no. Back in the old days we ran together, Harv and me and the Younger boys. Robbed a few banks together, a train here and there, but then I decided to get out of the business."

"And become a lawman."

"Nah, I wanted a pillow under my head o' nights, so I married a widder woman with a simple son, and for a while, we prospered in the dry goods trade. Then she took up with a corsets drummer behind my back. When I found out, I got so damn mad I put a bullet in the drummer—his name was Maxwell T. Dinwiddie—and damn near killed the little son of a bitch."

Jolly used his pinkie finger to knock ash off his cigar. "Well, the wife left me after that and I drifted into the Indian Territory. Killed a man in fair fight in Stillwater and another in an unfair fight in Oklahoma City and got arrested. But Judge Parker offered me a choice—a badge or George Maledon's noose. I took the badge."

"I can't let you go after the Fat Man, Marshal," Drake said.

Jolly's eyes hardened. "Don't tell Washita Jolly what he can't do, boy."

"Thornton will kill Nancy as soon as he sees you coming."

"Then he won't see me coming until it's too late."

"I'm riding with you, Marshal."

"Suit yourself. Glad to have you along." Suddenly Jolly didn't look like a lawman; he looked like the hard-faced outlaw who once rode with the Youngers. "But if it comes down to it, I'll step over your sweetheart's skun body to get to the Fat Man. Understand?"

"Yeah, Marshal, I guess I do."

"Good. I like to make myself understood," Jolly said.

Chapter 53

"Damn rain," Jolly grumbled. "I hate riding in the rain—another reason I quit the banking and railroad business. Seemed always to be raining when I was on the scout."

"You're the lawman," Drake said. "How do we play this?"

"Carefully. Despite what you think, I'm not keen to ride into Harv Thornton's gun."

"Give me a clue, Marshal."

"All right, then we dog his back trail and wait for an opportunity."

"What kind of opportunity?"

"Hell, Wayfarer, I don't know. But I'll know it when I see it." Jolly glanced at the surly sky. "Damn rain."

"I don't want Nancy harmed."

"How many times are you going to tell me that?"

"Until you get it stuck in your thick head, Marshal."

Jolly smiled. "Wayfarer, you're surely a tribulation to me. I've killed men for talking to me the way you do."

"And I'll kill any man who harms Nancy. Makes us even, doesn't it?"

The lawman's eyes iced over. "Go right on pushing it, boy. See what happens one of these times."

"I won't push it, Marshal. Just keep it in mind."

"You really love her, huh?"

"Yes, I really do."

"I've never loved a woman that much."

"Then you missed out on something wonderful."

"Damn it, boy, you sound like a woman your own self. Men don't say that word, 'wonderful.'"

"This one does, but it's real recent."

Jolly shook his head. "Wayfarer, you're a strange ranny."

They rode past Winding Stair Mountain, its crest and slopes and deep ravines covered with oak, hickory, and pine forests. The land smelled clean, of rain and the scouring wind, and the breath of trees.

An hour later Drake, riding point, found the freight wagon abandoned in the middle of a creek, its rear axle splintered.

Jolly rode beside the wagon and lifted the canvas. "What the hell does he have in there? A house?"

"Yeah," Drake said, "a portable cabin for the Fat Man. All it's doing is slowing them down, so they didn't make any attempt to repair the axle."

He looked at Jolly, a realization dawning on him. "The Fat Man is stuck in his armored wagon. I figure there's only four of his men left and it would take a dozen to lift him out of there."

"How heavy is that wagon thing?"

"I don't know, but it's heavy, steel plates all over it."

"And he's still got the Kiamichi River to cross," Jolly said. "It's low at this time of year, but all this damned rain may have it swollen and showing white water."

"You're seeing an opportunity, Marshal?"

"If they're busy getting an armored wagon across a swollen river, they may not guard their prisoners so close."

Drake weighed their chances in his mind, balancing the benefits against the risks. Finally he said, "It sounds like the best chance we'll have."

"Maybe, but I'm a careful man, Wayfarer. Only if it looks real good will we risk it."

"You thinking about the prisoners or Thornton?" Drake said.

"Thornton," Jolly said without even a moment's hesitation. "He's too good with a gun to ignore, so it all depends on him—where he's at and what he's doing."

"Maybe I can take him," Drake said.

"Wayfarer, put that damned thought out of your head. You wouldn't even come close."

"And you, Marshal?"

"I got two speeds on the draw, slow and slower."

"Does Thornton know that?"

"Damn right he does."

Drake and Jolly camped that night in Devils Hollow, a treed, bowl-shaped depression that hid the light of their fire.

They were on the trail again just after dawn, following the track of the armored wagon south across rolling hill country.

The rain had stopped, but the sky was gray mixed

with a few lighter clouds, the color of old bone. Thunder cracked to the north, back in the direction of the Winding Stair, and lightning flickered, close enough to shimmer along the gaunt angles of Drake's face.

"I reckon the river's about three miles ahead of us," Jolly said. He slid a Winchester out of the boot under his knee. "Ride heads up and eyes sharp, Wayfarer. Be prepared."

But nothing Drake did could adequately prepare him for the grotesque horror that lay in front of him and an entity so vile that he could only gape at its existence and wonder how God could create a creature so monstrous.

Chapter 54

About a half mile north of the river, Drake and Jolly found the spot where the armored wagon had stopped, presumably while Thornton looked for a suitable place to cross.

The tracks then led north for a hundred yards before swinging into a natural break in the trees where they headed toward the river again.

Both banks of the Kiamichi were heavily wooded, offering plenty of cover, and both riders were able to stay mounted as they approached the water.

To Drake's disappointment, the river was not swollen to any extent. The point where the wagon had crossed was marked by a wide sandbank, a narrow, sluggish stream flowing along each side of it. There was no white water.

Both men dismounted on the far bank and went the rest of the way on foot, before going to cover among the hickories and oaks.

What Drake saw on the opposite bank stunned him,

and even Jolly looked like a man experiencing a sight he'd never expected to witness.

The surviving oxen had been unhitched, and the entire left side of the wagon and been swung downward, forming a ramp.

Thornton and a couple of his men stood near the bottom of the ramp, rifles across their chests. The gunmen grinned as they watched the two women carry buckets of water from the river.

Nancy and Helen Lee threw the water into the wagon, then walked back to the river to refill them while Rockefeller scrubbed the inside with a straw broom.

"What the hell is that stench?" Jolly whispered, his nose wrinkled.

"That's the stink of the Fat Man," Drake said. "Nancy calls it the smell of evil."

Jolly shook his head. "That's not what I would call it." He elbowed Drake, his jaw slack. "Look, over there by the cottonwood. Hell, would you look at that . . ."

It had once been human, the massive, naked creature propped up against a cottonwood. There was nothing of the masculine form left, only a vast mountain of fat supported by what were once legs but were now pillars of sagging, filthy flesh. The belly hung over the thighs like a sack of grain, so pendulous it almost scraped the ground. Hair, long, black, and matted spread over round, monstrous shoulders, and the untrimmed fingernails of both hands had become clawed, black talons.

Drake, repulsed by the sight, yet fascinated, wondered how the Fat Man had transformed himself from human to monster. He had seen no sign of food in the man's cabin, nor had he ever seen his guards feed him.

The Fat Man was sick, physically, mentally, and emotionally, and that could be the only explanation.

Beside him stood the Chinese girl, small, slender, and frail, her head bowed, taking no interest in anything around her.

A reinforced iron cot with a filthy mattress had been carried away from the wagon and abandoned near the tree line.

As Drake watched, Thornton took a full bucket from Helen Lee's hands. He stood in front of the Fat Man and tossed the cold river water over him.

Thornton grinned, reached under his slicker, and produced a horse brush. He shook the Chinese girl, then handed her the brush, making scrubbing motions, pointing to the Fat Man.

Without even glancing at Thornton, the girl began to scrub the man's chest. The Fat Man roared and tried to swing at the girl's head.

Thornton thought this highly amusing, and Drake heard him laugh out loud and holler, "I always wanted to scrub your dirty hide, Fat Man!"

Drake was puzzled. Thornton had always treated the Fat Man with deference. What had happened? Why was he suddenly abusing him that way, with a cruelty he obviously relished?

It was something to do with the defeat at Green Meadow, he was certain. But what?

Beside Drake, Jolly was grinning. "Hell, Wayfarer," he said, "I can end this right here and the hell with the judge."

He brought his rifle to his shoulder.

"No!" Drake said. "The Fat Man can't be kill—"

The rifle blasted.

Instantly the Chinese girl cried out and fell, sudden blood blossoming on the back of her head.

"Damn it, she moved," Jolly said.

Then, more attuned to approaching danger than Drake, he said, "Quick, Wayfarer, into the trees. Don't let Harv see you."

Drake caught the lawman's drift at once, and melted back into the hickories.

Thornton dusted the trees with his rifle, aiming in the direction of the smoke drift.

"Drake, you son of a bitch, now your ladylove gets skun," he yelled.

Before Drake even thought of replying, Jolly yelled, "It's me, Harv. Washita Jolly, as ever was."

A long pause as Thornton considered that, then, "Show yourself."

From his hiding place in the brush, Drake saw Jolly step out of the trees, his rifle ready across his chest.

"What the hell are you doing here?" Thornton asked. He walked to the edge of the riverbank. "Is that little shit Chauncey Drake with you?"

"Who's he?"

"A one-handed man, acts real uppity."

"Can't say I've had the pleasure, Harv. I only want the Fat Man. Judge Parker has a notion to hang him."

Thornton grinned. "You'll need a ship's cable for the drop, Washita."

"If that's what it takes, Harv."

"Well, you can't have him. And don't try to shoot him again. You're lucky you hit the girl." Thornton grinned. "You never could shoot worth a damn, Washita."

"Why not give him to me, Harv? He means nothing to you, and he's done."

"Maybe so. But he's got a safe full of money in this here wagon, and I mean to get the combination from him."

"Hell, Harv, just blow the damn thing and give me the Fat Man."

"The safe's too big. If I use all the dynamite it would take, the money and other stuff inside will be blown to kingdom come."

"I see your problem, Harv."

"Yeah, and now you're a problem, Washita."

"You mean to shoot it out with me, Harv?"

"If I have to. But for old time's sake, you can turn around and go back to Fort Smith."

"Can we bargain, Harv?"

"For what?"

"Don't turn me away empty-handed, Harv. Give me the three people you're holding hostage and I'll head back to Fort Smith."

Thornton grinned. "Not a chance, Washita. I'm keeping the women for myself, and the man is worth money, billions he says."

"Then we have nothing else to say to each other."

"You summed it up, Washita. Now light a shuck. Come around again, and I'll kill one of the women. Or you."

"I'm leaving. I'll see you again, Harv."

"Hey, and if you meet that one-handed man, tell him I'm keeping his woman. She wants me more than him anyhow."

"I'll tell him if I see him, Harv."

Jolly turned and walked back into the trees, looking straight ahead, being careful to ignore Drake.

But Drake stayed where he was.

He wasn't through here yet, not by a long shot.

Chapter 55

After the Chinese girl was shot, Nancy ran to her. She knelt beside her and cradled the girl's head in her lap.

Thornton now stepped beside them and poked at the girl with the muzzle of his rifle.

Drake couldn't hear what the man was saying, but it seemed to indicate that the Chinese girl was dead.

His guess was confirmed when Nancy gently laid the girl's head on the ground and got to her feet.

Thornton's third man appeared from the trees, carrying a load of firewood and kindling, and the big gunman beckoned him over. He said something to the man and watched while he piled the wood under the wagon.

Thornton bent, inspected the wood, and grinned, seemingly satisfied with what he saw. The rain had stopped and the wood would stay tinder dry.

He grinned, slapped the man on the back, then said a few more words to him. The gunman nodded, then walked up the ramp into the wagon. He reappeared carrying a can with a wire handle and spout, and he had coiled ropes around his shoulder.

The man jumped off the side of the ramp and left the coal oil beside the wood. He handed a rope to Thornton and the other gunmen, then waved Rockefeller over.

At first Rockefeller refused to take a rope, but a rifle butt driven between his shoulder blades soon convinced him otherwise.

Four loops were placed over the Fat Man's head and under his armpits, two on each side of him. Thornton and the other men took up the slack, then hauled on the ropes.

At first the Fat Man did not move.

Then he suddenly came to life, cursing at the top of his voice as he tried to get out of the loops.

Thornton and the others jerked on the ropes. Drake could make out Rockefeller's features, frozen into an expression of horror.

The Fat Man toddled forward a few steps, his huge rolls of fat jiggling, then crashed facedown on the ground.

Drake heard Thornton yell, "Pull the fat bastard!"

The gunman and the other three retreated to the ramp, hauling on the Fat Man. The gross body inched forward across the muddy ground. After another fifteen minutes of struggle, the Fat Man, scratched and bloody, was finally dragged onto the ramp.

At an order from Thornton, the four men dropped the ropes and rested, hands on their hips, breathing hard.

He yelled something to the women and Helen Lee brought a canteen. Thornton took a drink and passed it to the others.

The Fat Man was lying on his back, a naked mass of flesh, fish belly white except where rocks and tree roots had left gouges on his skin.

Thornton's back was to Drake, but he thought he

was saying something to the Fat Man, who kept shaking his head.

Now the gunman looked at the others and gave an order. A man moved beside Thornton so that there were two men on each side of the ramp.

"Lift!" Thornton yelled.

But four men could not lift the steel-armored door high enough to get it closed. By mutual consent they stepped back and let the ramp thud back onto the ground and the Fat Man, screaming, rolled off onto his gargantuan belly.

Again the ropes were used to drag the Fat Man back onto the ramp. But this time Thornton ordered Rockefeller and the others inside the wagon and all four men pulled from there.

The great body barely moved.

Thornton yelled a command and Nancy got the coal oil can. The gunmen and Rockefeller stopped hauling while she poured oil onto the ramp.

At another word from Thornton the girl stopped, and the men began pulling again.

This time the Fat Man slid more easily and, an inch at a time, he was hauled up the ramp and flopped like a stranded whale into the wagon.

Led by Thornton, the men jumped from the wagon to the ground, and this time lifted the ramp more easily.

But Thornton stopped them.

He stepped to the Chinese girl's body and, like a man carrying a rag doll, effortlessly took her back to the wagon and tossed her inside.

Even at a distance, Drake heard the gunman's triumphant yell. "Company for you, Fat Man! Now do you remember the numbers for the safe?"

Drake didn't hear the Fat Man's answer but it was easy enough to guess, because Thornton cursed loud and long. The ramp clanged into place, again becoming one of the wagon's armored sides.

The gunmen slammed home the six outside bolts; then one of them grabbed the coal oil can and poured the contents over the wood and kindling under the wagon.

Thornton thumbed a match into life and threw it onto the wood, which immediately blazed into flame.

"No!" Rockefeller roared.

He ran at Thornton, his fists swinging. The big gunman easily avoided Rockefeller's wild punches and hit him hard in the gut. As Rockefeller doubled over, Thornton brought up his knee, smashing it into the older man's face.

Blood spurting from his mouth and nose, Rockefeller fell, stretched his length on the ground and lay still.

Always a man to kick an enemy when he's down, Thornton booted Rockefeller in the ribs, stepped away, but came back and delivered another kick.

Jolly got down on one knee beside Drake. "I took the horses back a ways out of sight," he said. He looked across the river. "What's happening?"

"Well, John D. just got Thornton's knee in his face."

"That hurts."

"I guess it does. And they're trying to roast the Fat Man alive. He's in the wagon with the dead Chinese girl."

Jolly shook his head. "I surely regret that shot."

"So does she, I'm sure."

Ten minutes later the Fat Man uttered his first scream.

Chapter 56

Harvey Thornton let out an exultant whoop. He jumped onto a rear wagon wheel and yelled into the barred window at the top of the wagon.

"Let's hear another one, Fat Man!"

He didn't have to wait long, as another terrified shriek echoed from the wagon.

"You remember them numbers now?" Thornton hollered.

Jolly was fingering his rifle, his predatory eyes on Thornton.

"The man has the luck of the devil," he said. "I can't get a clear shot. Damned tree's in the way."

"If you're not certain, don't take the shot," Drake said. "I don't want Nancy joining the Chinese girl in the wagon."

"When he steps down from the wheel . . ."

"No!" Drake said. "It's too risky. You can miss, Jolly."

The marshal nodded. "At this range, shooting across a river, yeah, I can miss."

"Listen!" Drake said.

"You sure that's the numbers?" Thornton yelled, his mouth against the small window. "If you're lying to me Fat Man, I'll roast you alive."

Another scream, louder, full of pain and fear.

"You men, stand by with the buckets," Thornton shouted. "Jake, douse the fire."

The gunman jumped down from the wagon wheel and slammed the bolts open. "Stand back!" he yelled.

The armored door crashed to the ground, bounced once, then stopped.

Thornton and his men tossed buckets of water inside, and immediately a hissing cloud of steam billowed from the wagon.

The gunman ordered one of his men to get more water. "We got to wet down the damned safe to get it open," he yelled.

Beside Drake, Washita Jolly grinned. He raised his rifle to his shoulder. "Now I can nail the son of a bitch," he said.

Drake's worried eyes darted to Thornton.

The man's form was hazy behind the steam, and he was moving around, constantly yelling to his men. It was not an easy shot. Refusing to take the chance, mentally thanking the gods that Jolly was on his left side, Drake drew his Colt and slammed it hard into the marshal's forehead, just above the top of the Winchester.

Jolly did not utter a sound. He toppled like a felled pine and landed on his back. He lay there unmoving, his mouth open, eyes rolling in his head, drool trickling down his chin.

"I told you not to try a shot," Drake said. "People could get hurt."

Jolly groaned and said nothing.

Delighted yells rang out from across the river.

Thornton ran down the ramp, bundles of money in each hand. Behind him, his two men carried canvas bags, heavy with coin.

What happened next came with the speed of a striking rattler and left Drake with a breath stuck in his throat like a dry chicken bone.

Thornton dropped the money in his right hand and skinned his Colt. Two shots. Two dead men. Two women screaming. Thornton grinning.

A few minutes later, his saddlebags bulging, Thornton rode out with the two women. He left his dead where they lay, and Rockefeller on his hands and knees, strings of blood leaking from his shattered mouth.

The Fat Man was screaming again.

Drake rose to his feet just as Washita Jolly stirred.

The marshal looked up at him. "Wha . . . what happened?"

"You don't remember?" Drake said, taking a knee beside the prone lawman.

"Something hit me on the head. I remember you trying to protect me, pushing me down."

"You'll be all right, Marshal," Drake said. "You were grazed by a stray bullet, that's all."

"Was it Thornton?"

"Could be. Those boys were celebrating over there, banging off guns. But Thornton ended the festivities by shooting both of them."

"He's gone?"

"Yeah, emptied the Fat Man's safe first. Then he rode out. Took the women with him."

Jolly tried to struggle to a sitting position. Drake helped him.

"My brains are scrambled, Wayfarer," Jolly said, rubbing the bump on his head. "I dreamed you buffaloed me."

"Could be. I had my gun in my hand when I tried to push you out of the line of fire. The barrel of my Colt was probably the last thing you saw before the bullet hit."

"Help me to my feet, Chauncey. I'm calling you Chauncey on account of how you saved my life." Jolly swayed then steadied, his hand on Drake's shoulder. "Banging off guns, you say?"

"Yeah, Marshal. When they started shooting across the river, that's when I pushed you back. Just as well, your head could have been blowed clean off."

"I'm beholden to you, Chauncey," Jolly said. There was a tear in his eye.

"Glad I was around to help, Marshal."

Jolly started, looking across the river. "What the hell was that?"

"The Fat Man screaming, I reckon."

"We'd better get over there, Chauncey. Bring the horses quick. He might still be well enough to hang."

Chapter 57

Drake and Jolly dismounted close to the wagon.

The Fat Man was still screaming, and when Drake looked inside the reason was plain.

The smell of scorched flesh told part of the story; the slim body of the Chinese girl sprawled on top of the man told the rest.

The Fat Man's eyes were popping out of his head. When he saw Drake and the marshal, he babbled, "Her head's blown away, but she talked to me . . . told me how much she hated me . . . told me I'd burn in hell. Is this hell? I'm burning bad. Am I in hell?"

"Damn it, Chauncey, look at his back."

The flesh of the Fat Man's back had bubbled from heat when he'd been stuck to the red-hot floor of the wagon.

"He smells like a roasting pig," Jolly said.

"Help me," the Fat Man said. "Take me to Texas and I'll make both of you rich men. Get this bitch off of me. She's still talking . . . talking . . ."

The girl's face was still in death and at first Drake

thought she could be asleep. But then he saw that part of her brain had been blown out by Jolly's bullet.

"I'm taking her out of there," Drake said. "She'd had enough of the Fat Man when she was alive."

He climbed into the wagon and lifted the girl off the man's gross body. She was so light and frail carrying her in one arm was no handicap.

The marshal, displaying a tenderness that surprised Drake, took the girl from him and gently laid her on the grass, covering her with his slicker.

Jolly drew his gun and waved it at the Fat Man. "You, get out of there."

"Marshal, he can't move," Drake said. "He's stuck to the iron."

"I'm in hell!" the Fat Man screamed. "Look, there she is again." He raised a massive arm and pointed at the steel wall of the wagon. "The Chinese bitch is coming for me. She's going to drag me down into the fiery pit with her."

"Take your medicine," Jolly said. "You're the baddest man that ever was."

But the Fat Man wasn't listening. He would never listen to anything ever again.

His eyes bugged like boiled eggs and he clutched frantically at his chest, his mouth opening in a soundless scream . . . and at that moment death took him by the ear.

The Fat Man greeted his terrible eternity with his eyes popping out of his head and a scream on his lips.

"Ticker gave out, damn him," Jolly said. "I surely wanted to see him hang." He studied the massive body, made even more grotesque by death. "How the hell do we bury that?"

"We don't," Drake said. "Let the coyotes have at it, and the others."

Rockefeller, his mouth covered in blood, had finally staggered to his feet. "Lay the girl to rest," he said. "She deserves that consideration."

Drake nodded. "Yes, she does." He looked at Rockefeller. "How do you feel, John?"

Rockefeller wiped away blood with the back of his hand. "How do you think I feel?"

"That was no way to treat a billionaire," Jolly said, smiling with as much sympathy as he could muster. "Remember I said that, Mr. Rockefeller."

Despite the fact that he was hurting bad, the instincts of a gentleman had not deserted Rockefeller.

"I see you're wounded yourself, mister . . . ?"

"Jolly, sir. Washita Jolly, deputy marshal out of Judge Isaac Parker's court."

"Pleased to meet you, Marshal Jolly. That's a nasty head wound, indeed."

As Drake looked at the ground and shuffled his feet, Jolly said, "I got grazed by a bullet. Chauncey here saved my life."

"It could only have been fired by Thornton," Rockefeller said. "Though I fail to see how—"

"Washita, we got a burying to do," Drake said quickly. "There are shovels tied to the back of the wagon."

They buried the girl deep, and Rockefeller said Christian words, having no idea how the Chinese laid their dead to rest.

After Jolly replaced his hat, he looked across the grave at Drake and said, "This is the end of the line for me, Chauncey. I'm heading back to Fort Smith."

"It's not over yet," Drake said. "Thornton is still alive."

Jolly shook his head. "I was ordered to effect the arrest of the Fat Man. Well, he's dead and there's an end to it. As for Harvey Thornton, the judge has no interest in him at this time. Hell, Chauncey, he's pinned badges on worse."

The marshal looked at Rockefeller. "Mr. Rockefeller, I can take you back to Fort Smith with me. You can get a train connection to most anywhere from there."

"Thank you kindly, Marshal, but I'm staying with Mr. Drake, I mean Chauncey."

Jolly sighed. "Looking at your split lips and black eyes, I reckon you got reason enough. But going after Thornton will be a hard trail, and dangerous."

"I'll take my chances, Marshal." Rockefeller turned to Drake. "Will you have me along, Chauncey?"

"Honored to have you, John."

"Then it's settled."

Jolly stepped into the saddle and looked down at the two men. "Good luck," he said. "You two pilgrims are going to need it." He smiled at Drake. "Chauncey, I know you saved my life an' all, but you won't forget my seventy-nine dollars and fifty cents, will you?"

"Washita, it's engraved on my heart."

The marshal touched his hat. "I hope I see you boys around some time."

He swung his horse to the north and crossed the river and rode into the trees.

"A fine police officer," Rockefeller said after Jolly was gone from sight.

"A prince among men," Drake said.

Chapter 58

The rain had stopped again, but there was no celebration of blue sky and singing birds. Iron gray clouds still threatened, hinting darkly at things to come, and in the meantime the wind took up the slack, tossing the trees, scattering roosting crows like scraps of charred paper.

Rockefeller was mounted on his own horse, sitting his saddle head bent, busy with his own thoughts. Drake was content to ride in silence, though the pain in his left hand chided him constantly and gave him no peace.

The passage of three shod horses leaves scars on the land, and Drake had no difficulty following Thornton's trail. He prayed for the rain to stay away and not erase the tracks.

Three miles after leaving the river, Drake and Rockefeller entered the Kiamichi Mountain range, a heavily forested region of high, rawboned ridges and deep canyons.

The trail south led past Smith Ridge, then the pine

and hickory slopes of Dutchman Ridge, standing fifteen hundred feet above the flat.

After a three-hour ride through the Kiamichi peaks, Drake and Rockefeller left the rolling country and entered a narrow valley cut through by the headwaters of the Little River.

At this time of the year the river was little more than a sandy stream. But here they lost Thornton's trail and were forced to scout the rocky south bank for an hour before they picked up sign again.

Drake swung out of the saddle, picked up a ball of horse dung, and crumbled it between his fingers.

"It's fairly fresh," he said. "I'm not the best tracker in the west, but I figure they passed this way no more than a couple of hours ago."

He stood and looked into the distance.

The tracks were headed into a break in the low, treed Boktuklo Mountains. This was more difficult, rolling country that did not make for long riding.

"I reckon we can catch Thornton before sundown," Drake said.

"And what then?" Rockefeller said.

"Then we find out just how fast Thornton really is."

"From all I hear he's fast all right, Chauncey. Do we stand a chance?"

"I don't know. All we can do is take our hits and hope we're still standing when the smoke clears. You in favor of that, John?"

"No, not a bit. Are you?"

"No. And only a madman would be."

Drake looked up at Rockefeller, who looked even more gaunt and skinny than he remembered. "Maybe it's good that I'm crazy."

Rockefeller smiled. "Then I must be crazy too. Otherwise I wouldn't be here."

"Then we got it to do," Drake said.

He stepped into the saddle and headed his horse south.

It started to drizzle again.

The rain was not heavy but it brought with it a mist that shrouded the trail ahead and hung like smoke on the ridges, ghosting the tall pines.

Drake slowed his horse to a walk, picking his way as he bent over in the saddle and tried to read the ground.

He picked up tracks again just south of Wildhorse Mountain, and rode into lower grass and tree country, cut through by many shallow creeks.

Thornton's tracks were cut plain on the grama grass, heading due south. After an hour Drake and Rockefeller rode up on Pine Creek—and the bodies of two dead men.

The men lay sprawled on the grass, their horses grazing nearby among a stand of cottonwoods.

Drake dismounted, hearing Rockefeller's rifle slide out of the scabbard.

Both men had been shot dead center in the chest. They were big, bearded men, long, matted hair spread out over the grass around their heads. They were roughly dressed, one wearing a filthy army greatcoat, his lips pulled back from rotten teeth in his last death agony.

Drake had seen their like before, riffraff up from the Texas border country, ready to kill, steal, and rape as the mood took them. And with men like these, the mood took them often.

Rockefeller kneed his horse closer. "Thornton?"

"That's my guess. Fat saddlebags and two pretty women were sure to attract scum like this. They picked on the wrong man, was all."

"Well, Chauncey, neither of us is pretty, but I'd say we're doing a good job of attracting their kinfolk," Rockefeller said, looking into the misty distance. "Got women and a wagon with them."

Three men riding mustangs spread out, putting a few yards of space between them. The wagon stopped and two slatternly women and a couple of children got down.

It looked to Drake that the women had seen this before, as though they were watching the first act of a play they knew would end in violence and death.

The three riders were as big, shaggy, and dirty as the dead men. The one in the middle, a gray beard spreading over his chest, looked like a biblical patriarch. But there the resemblance ended. The man's belted Colts and the Winchester carried upright on his thigh brought him right into the here and now.

As for Drake, he touched his tongue to his top lip and wished to be anywhere but here and now, and he was certain that went double for Rockefeller.

Over his shoulder, Drake said, "Be ready, John."

"For what?"

"Shooting, if it starts."

Rockefeller's voice was tight. "Maybe we can talk to them, tell them who murdered their kin."

"Yeah, maybe. But I don't reckon these boys are much for conversation."

The three riders stopped and sat their mounts, saying nothing, but their careful eyes were everywhere, hardly lingering on the dead men.

Drake dropped the reins and took a step forward, smiling.

"Howdy, boys, you come at a sad time," he said.

"For some," the graybeard said. "You kill them?"

"No, a man named Harvey Thornton did that. We're hunting him."

"You the law?"

"You could say that. We're riding scout for three companies of the Tenth Cavalry."

Without turning, graybeard said, "Jericho, check out their back trail."

"Sure thing, Pa."

The man swung his horse and cantered to the north, following Drake's horse tracks.

"Harvey Thornton. Heard that name afore," Pa said. "He's one o' them Texas draw fighters, gets his name in all the newspapers and the dime novel books."

The welcoming smile on Drake's lips was frozen and he let it melt into frown. "Yeah, he's famous, but he's a killer, no doubt about that."

He tried another tack. "The cavalry plan on taking him to Fort Smith to be hung at Judge Parker's convenience."

"You a friend of Parker's?"

"We have dinner together now and then."

Pa nodded. "Uh-huh. Parker is the mad dog who hung my son Jeremiah. That were a year ago. Was you having dinner with him then?"

"Well, most times it was lunch," Drake said. "Maybe just a sandwich."

He looked at Pa's granite block of a face, the cold, merciless black eyes, and knew he wasn't going to gab his way out of this fight.

A killing time was hurtling toward him like a runaway locomotive on a straight track, and he was powerless to stop it.

Chapter 59

The man called Jericho returned and shook his head. "Don't see no so'jers."

Pa's eyes went to Drake. "You lying to me, boy?"

Drake said nothing, and the man said, "Jericho, you got young eyes. Who's lying there?"

"Why, it's cousin Jed and cousin Mervin, Pa. I seen 'em plain when we first rode up."

"We didn't kill them," Drake said.

"Hell, sonny, I know that," Pa said. "So does Jericho and my other spawn, Masheck, here. Don't you, boys?"

Masheck's slack mouth stretched in a grin that displayed three teeth, all of them black. He looked at Drake. "Hell, mister, you don't have the sand to have took Jed an' Marvin. They was good with the iron."

"Well, I'm glad we got that settled," Drake said. "Now, will you give us the road?"

"Can't rightly do that," Pa said. "See, that's our kin lying there. An eye for an eye, a tooth for a tooth, as the Good Book says."

"Damn it, man, we didn't kill them."

"What Pa means," Masheck said, "is any eye for an eye, any tooth for a tooth."

"Then ride after Harvey Thornton, damn you."

Pa shook his head. "Trouble is, he's way down the trail a fur piece, and you boys is right here."

The old man's rifle slapped into place, leveled at Drake's belly.

"No hard feelings, boys, but we got to be moving on," he said. "And we'll be a-riding them good hosses you got."

John D. Rockefeller was an intelligent man with an eye to the main chance, and he'd quickly grasped the concept that, like business, there are no rules in a gunfight, except one: Always cheat to win.

He turned his head to his left and yelled, "Huzzah! The cavalry's here!"

Pa and his sons jerked their heads around and gave Drake the half second Rockefeller knew he needed. And it was all he needed.

His Colt was out and blasting before the three riders realized what had happened.

Pa was hit hard. He fell from the saddle, his rifle spinning away from him.

Masheck got his Colt skinned, but Rockefeller, shooting from the waist, dropped him with one shot.

Jericho screamed his anger. He fired at Drake, missed, steadied himself for another shot.

The element of surprise gone, Drake took up the gunfighter's stance, left foot behind his right heel, Colt extended at arm's length.

He and Jericho fired at the same moment.

His frightened mustang throwing him badly off balance, Jericho's shot went wide. Drake's did not. His bullet took the man low on his left cheek, blowing away part of his jawbone.

Still game despite his terrible wound, Jericho fired again. But he was done. The bullet kicked up mud at Drake's feet.

Rockefeller finished the man with a shot that crashed into his chest, and Jericho went to meet the brothers and sisters that had been his ancestors.

"You dirty son of a bitch!"

One of the women at the wagon raised a shotgun and cut loose.

The buckshot whirred over Drake's head. He grabbed the reins of his horse and swung into the saddle.

A rifle cracked and a bullet plowed into the dirt close to Rockefeller. The woman who had fired first was fumbling with bright red shells.

Drake kicked his mount into a run, Rockefeller close behind him. Bullets and buckshot chased after them, but the angry women scored no hits.

After a mile, Drake slowed to a walk and Rockefeller rode up beside him.

Drake looked at him. "We had no quarrel with those men."

"None. But their talking was done, and ours."

"Maybe I should have tried to talk longer, or better."

"Yes, better, I understand that now. It dawned on me back there, Chauncey, that the ability to deal with people is a purchasable commodity like sugar or coffee, and after this is over, I plan to pay more for that ability than for any other under the sun."

Drake smiled. "John D., you're a strange man."

"People have told me that."

"Have they also told you that you're a brave one?"

"Not that I recall."

"Well, you are."

Rockefeller was quiet for a while; then he grinned. "Damn right, I am."

Drake and Rockefeller reached the Cedar Mountains just before nightfall.

Thornton's tracks had long since been washed away by rain and Drake had headed due south, hoping that the gunman would have taken the same route.

The few travelers they met on the trail said they had seen nothing of a man and two women. There had also been no sign of the cavalry.

"How much longer do we give it, Chauncey?" Rockefeller said.

"As long as it takes."

The older man shook his head. "Tomorrow, Chauncey. If there's no sign of them I'm heading back."

Drake was not angry. "You have business interests, John. I understand."

"Let the soldiers find them," Rockefeller said. "Even three understrength companies would number around a hundred and twenty men. They can spread out and search a wider area than we could."

"I'm here, John. The soldiers aren't. I'll keep on going until I find Nancy."

Rockefeller, a resourceful man, had scavenged a pot and coffee from the Fat Man's camp. Now the coffee bubbled on the fire, a few strips of bacon sizzling on a stick.

They had camped in a grove of oaks where there

was grass for the horses and protection from the wind and rain, both of which had stopped for now, leaving a night of dead calm and dark quiet.

"I almost forgot, I got you something," Rockefeller said. He handed Drake the makings. "I remembered that you're a smoking man."

Smiling, Drake said, "You brought me a dead ranny's tobacco."

"It's from one of the men Thornton shot back at the Fat Man's wagon. I supposed he had no further use for it. Of course, if you don't want it, just toss it away. You won't hurt my feelings."

"Tobacco from a dead man tastes just as good as tobacco from a live one."

Drake rolled a cigarette and lit it from the fire.

"Change your mind, Chauncey," Rockefeller said. "Go back with me and look for the cavalry. Then you can go after Nancy with them."

Rockefeller looked at the dirty bandage around Drake's stumps. "And, if you don't mind me saying so, you badly need medical attention for that hand."

"It's all right. Doesn't hurt any. Well, not as much."

Rockefeller's eyes moved over Drake's face. "You're not going back, are you?"

"Nope, not until I free Nancy."

"You're a stubborn man."

"Seems like."

Rockefeller poured coffee for them both. Crimson firelight moving on his face, he said, "Tell me something, Chauncey."

"Sure. What do you want to know?"

"How did you get that fast with a gun?"

Drake smiled. "A man doesn't get that fast, John, he's born fast. Took me by surprise when I discovered it, I mean, that I was faster than most."

He tried his coffee. "A lot of Western men carry a gun but very few are fast on the draw, maybe one in a thousand. Like I said, you have to be born to it."

Drake looked down at tobacco and papers, preparing another cigarette. "You thinking of becoming a famous pistolero, John?"

Rockefeller laughed. "No, not really. I'm just curious about many things. Now, take the Chinese porcelain trade for example, I—"

The woman's voice rang out from the darkness like the call of a distant bugle.

"Don't shoot at me. I'm coming in."

Chapter 60

Drake rose to his feet, his hand close to his holstered Colt.

"You know the drill, lady," he yelled. "Slow and smiling, like you're visiting kin."

"It's me, Mr. Drake, Helen Lee."

"Is Nancy with you?"

"I'm alone."

Helen rode through the oaks, then drew rein. She swayed in the saddle and would have fallen to the ground had Rockefeller not caught her and carried her to the fire.

He helped Helen sit and supported her with an arm around her shoulders. "Chauncey," he said, "she needs coffee."

Helen Lee looked like she'd been through it.

Her face was bruised, there were dark circles under her eyes and when she looked at Drake, her gaze was as fragile as spun glass.

He passed the woman coffee. She placed hands

around the cup, held it close to her lips, but made no attempt to drink, as though the warmth brought her comfort.

"Tell us, Miss Lee," Rockefeller said. "And remember, you're talking to a friend, not your employer."

Helen took a breath, then said, "Thornton got drunk, very drunk, and I took a horse and rode away."

"When was that?" Drake asked.

"Last night."

"And you didn't take Nancy with you?" There was a hard edge to Drake's voice.

"No."

"Damn you. Why the hell not?"

"Chauncey, please, she's been through a lot," Rockefeller said.

Helen laid the cup beside her, and rested her forehead on her knees. She didn't look at Drake.

"Nancy is dead," she said, a thin whisper.

Drake leaned toward the woman, his face stricken.

"What the hell did you say?"

"She's dead, Chauncey. Nancy is dead."

"How?" The shock had left Drake dazed. "Tell—tell me—how—how?"

"Harvey Thornton killed her."

For long moments those four words lay between them like chunks of raw meat.

"He killed her?" Drake said finally. He shook his head, his eyes confused, questioning. "Why?"

Now Helen looked at him. "He wanted her. She couldn't take that, a man raping her again, and she fought him."

The woman's face revealed the mental battle she was fighting. "Chauncey, you don't want to hear this."

Suddenly Drake was as cold as ice. He sat still, unmoving as a block of granite.

"I want to hear it, all of it."

"Thornton was drunk. He started cursing her, then pounded on her with his fists. Nancy was such a little thing, fragile. She screamed just once. Then . . . Well, then she died."

Drake's hollow voice sounded as though he was talking from inside a tomb. He took his time asking the question, spacing his words.

"Where . . . is . . . he?"

"Chauncey, let Thornton be," Helen said. "He's a demon with a gun. He'll kill you."

"Where . . . is . . . he?"

"Tell him, Miss Lee," Rockefeller said. "It's the man's right."

"South of here, maybe fifteen, twenty miles," Helen said. "You won't catch him before he reaches the Red, and he has many friends in Texas."

She laid her hand on Drake's. "Let the law bring him to justice, Chauncey. Don't throw your life away. Nancy wouldn't want that."

Drake rose to his feet. Then, as though he hadn't heard, he said, "John, I want your horse."

"What are you going to do, Chauncey?" Rockefeller asked.

"Do? I'm going to hunt Thornton down, and if I have to kill two horses doing it, I will."

Rockefeller had learned something about Western men, that when they figure their talking is done, they'll act, and nothing on God's green earth will stop them.

He didn't argue, knowing how futile that would be. "I'll saddle the horses," he said.

Left alone with Drake, Helen Lee said, "We'll be waiting for you when you get back." She gave him a kind of sad little smile. "We've come a long way from that first night in Green Meadow."

Drake nodded. "Seems like. And I still have a long ways to go."

The woman stood and extended her hand. "Good luck, Mr. Drake. I don't have the words to tell you how I feel about Nancy."

"I can see it in your eyes. They say enough."

After a few minutes Rockefeller led in the horses. His long Yankee face was worried.

"Can you take him, Chauncey?"

"I don't think so."

"But you have to do this thing? No, wait—don't answer that," Rockefeller said. "I know you have to do it."

Like Helen before him, he held out his hand.

"Good luck, Chauncey."

Drake smiled and said nothing.

Leading Rockefeller's horse, he rode into the night.

The coyotes were calling close, their cries echoing across a land made black and silver by a blood moon.

Chapter 61

Chauncey Drake rode through the rest of the night and into the following day. He abandoned his own horse at the Little River and mounted Rockefeller's big stud.

He estimated he was only six miles north of the Red and must be closing fast on Thornton.

If he could find him.

To the south lay a vast area of oak forest that stretched almost to the river, where a man could lose himself forever if he had a mind.

But Thornton had no idea he was being followed, and an outlaw with money will look for opportunities to spend it.

The man might be close, over the next rise or the one after that.

Drake kneed the stud forward, moving through a gray dawn light, aware that he'd spent the night riding under a blood moon, always unlucky for him.

But good luck often comes to a man who does not include it in his plans. And so it did for Chauncey Drake.

Just before noon, he topped a treed hogback and rode

down to Mud Creek, only six miles from the Texas border. To his surprise, there was a small settlement sprawled along the south bank, set among cottonwoods.

The place was not much, a rundown annex of hell consisting of a dugout saloon, a few cabins and corrals, and a low adobe building that served as a combination general store and hotel.

That was Drake's initial impression, but after he crossed the river and rode closer he realized his mistake. It was not a hotel but a hog ranch, judging by the three unkempt women who sat on a wooden bench to the left of the door and appraised him with bold, calculating glances. Nearby, a couple of naked, dirty children played in the dirt among pecking chickens and threw clods of mud at a sleeping, spotted dog.

But what attracted Drake's attention was the fine horse at the hitching rail outside the saloon, an animal worth more than the entire settlement.

Along the border country only outlaws and lawmen owned good horses—men like Harvey Thornton.

Drake stepped out of the leather and eased out his Colt. He slid a round into the empty chamber under the hammer and reholstered the revolver.

He had not gotten a good look at Thornton's mount when he rode away from the Fat Man's wagon. It could be his, or somebody's else's, maybe even a Ranger's, so walking into the saloon with gun drawn and murder in his eye was probably not a good idea.

Gathering the reins, Drake led his horse toward the hitching rail.

Then stopped dead in his tracks, as surprised as the man who's just bumped into his mother-in-law in a brothel.

The saloon door crashed open and slammed against the wall on its rawhide hinges and Harvey Thornton backed out, gun blazing.

There was a scream from inside; then a man was suddenly framed in the doorway. He and Thornton fired at the same time. The man seemed to shrink in on himself, his knees buckled, and he slid down the wall to a sitting position, head lolling on his chest, as dead as he was ever going to be.

Drake took a single sidestep, drawing his Colt.

"Thornton!" he yelled.

The gunman turned, saw Drake, and snarled his anger. His gun came up and he fired. But just as he triggered the shot, the spotted dog, now figuring him for an enemy, jumped at him.

Off balance, Thornton's bullet went wide.

Drake fired. A clean miss.

Thornton kicked the dog away from him and untied his horse from the rail. He turned the animal so that it was between him and Drake, then ran alongside for a few yards before vaulting into the saddle.

Drake fired, aiming for the horse, a bigger target, fired again. Cursing, he climbed into the leather and went after Thornton.

Behind him, women wailed and children cried, their lives shattered by a visit from a widowmaker who knew neither mercy nor a whisper of conscience.

Thornton drew rein at the edge of the oak forest, looked around him, then plunged ahead into the trees. Drake followed, taking the same game trail.

There was no wind and the sun slanted through the tree canopies like light from cathedral windows, the silence so profound a man alone might sing, "Carve Dat Possum," to end the agony of the quiet.

But Chauncey Drake was not alone.

Ahead of him he heard the drum of Thornton's horse. The gunman was not afraid of any man and Drake wondered when he would turn and make his stand.

Drake's eyes were fixed on the trees, aware that Thornton might set an ambush. A picture popped into his head, one he'd seen in a book, of a stone knight lying on a cathedral floor, his legs crossed and a dog at his feet.

He could end up like that at any moment, dead as a stone warrior, the bladed morning light shining on him.

The vision troubled Drake and he slowed his horse to a walk. If Thornton was laying for him he was not going to oblige him by charging into his gun.

He could no longer hear hoof beats, and that meant either the man was already far ahead of him or he'd stopped.

Drake stepped from the saddle and drew his gun. The forest hush unnerved him. Crickets played their small music in the grass and bees droned, but there was no birdsong. And nothing moved.

Leading his horse, Drake advanced along the game trail, following in Thornton's tracks.

After a hundred yards, the trail ended at a small clearing, bright with wildflowers. Above Drake was a patch of blue sky and the morning had turned hot.

Thornton's horse lay dead at the opposite edge of the clearing and the big gunman lay sprawled on his back beside it.

The shots Drake had fired at the horse had taken effect. It had run for a while and then dropped dead in its tracks.

Drake dropped the reins and stepped toward Thornton. "I hope you broke your damned fool neck," he said.

But Thornton stirred, groaned, and tried to sit up. Drake removed the gunman's hat, then slammed the barrel of his Colt hard against his head.

Thornton made no sound. He toppled onto his right side and lay still.

Drake smiled. "Sleep tight, Harv."

Now he had work to do.

Chapter 62

Harvey Thornton did not stir while Drake stripped him naked, and for a moment he feared that he'd killed the man. But Thornton was still breathing and now and again his eyelids fluttered.

Drake checked the loads in his Colt, making sure he had five. He then took Thornton's gun and reloaded it.

Ten rounds.

It had been many years since he'd been a puncher, and Drake had no rope, neither was there one on Thornton's saddle.

"Then we do this the hard way, Harv," he said.

At that moment Drake was not entirely sane. The man who had beaten the woman he loved to death with his fists lay helpless at his feet. And that can plunge any man into madness.

A yellow and black butterfly flitted around Drake's head as he spread Thornton's arms wide, palms up.

He stepped on the gunman's left wrist, then his right, pinning him to the ground.

The pain penetrated Thornton's consciousness and

he woke, like a drowsy man returning from a deep sleep.

"What the . . . What the hell are you doing, Drake?" he said. He raised his head and looked down at his body. "I'm naked as a jaybird."

"It's payback time, Harv. And I'm charging you interest."

Thornton struggled, arched his back and tried to kick at his tormentor. But his wrists were firmly planted and he couldn't move effectively.

"Damn you, Chauncey," he said. "Let me go or I'll kill you."

Drake shook his head. "Your killing days are done, Harv. You'll never again beat a woman to death or gun some farm boy in a saloon."

A flash of fear showed in Thornton's eyes, but was replaced by a fox's cunning. "Chauncey, I've got twenty thousand in my saddlebags. We can share the money, you and me, keep us going in whiskey and women for years."

"Her name was Nancy, Harv. She never had a life, but I planned on giving her one." Drake smiled. "Can you say her name?"

"Damn you, what do I care what the bitch was called? Down there, Chauncey, in Texas, we can have all the women we need. Hell, we can screw them until we're glutted and then come back for more."

"You answered that question all wrong, Harv. Now you'll have to shuck your fear and take your medicine."

"I'll kill you, Chauncey. By God, I'll kill you."

Drake leaned over, shot once. Thornton's left thumb disintegrated.

It took a moment for the full horror of what had just happened to dawn on Thornton. When it did, he screamed, "Take it all. Take all the money. It's yours."

Drake fired again.

"Nancy, her name was Nancy," Thornton shrieked. "Damn you! Damn her! The name was Nancy."

Drake fired, taking his time, five shots in all.

He holstered his Colt, took Thornton's gun from his waistband, and started over, this time on the man's right hand.

Five shots.

Thornton was raving, saliva bubbling from his mouth as he writhed on the grass.

Drake nodded. "Well-done, Harv, you got the answer right in the end. Her name was Nancy."

He got off Thornton's wrists and stepped back a few yards.

The gunman staggered to his feet, staring at his ruined hands, his face stricken. "Why, you bastard?" he said.

"For this, Harv," Drake said, holding up his mangled left. "And because you're not worth killing."

"Damn you, finish me."

"No. I'll let you do that yourself, or leave it to the first wannabe gunslinger who hankers to be known as the man who shot Harvey Thornton." Drake pointed to the south. "Texas is that way."

He walked to Thornton's dead horse and stripped away the saddlebags. Then he turned his back on the gunman and stepped into the saddle.

"Damn you, what will I do?" Thornton said. He was almost in tears, all his gunman's arrogance vanished, gone like smoke in the wind.

"You'll live or you'll die, Harv," Drake said. "I don't much care either way."

"At least leave me a gun."

"Harv, you can't hold a gun anymore, remember?"

Thornton screamed, and he was still screaming as Drake rode through the forest, where up until recently a holy silence had lain among the trees.

To his surprise, Drake's horse had not wandered far and he found it after only an hour of search.

He reached the camp in the Cedar Mountain well before nightfall and insisted on coffee before he told Rockefeller and Helen Lee about his encounter with Thornton.

After he'd finished, he said, "Now I have to return this money."

Rockefeller was surprised. "Return it? Return it to whom? The Fat Man's ill-gotten gains came from all over the world. God knows how much more he has stashed away in banks from here to China."

Drake thought that through, then said, "I guess you have a point. If I returned it to the law all I'd do is make some town marshal rich."

"How much money is involved?" Rockefeller asked.

"About twenty thousand."

Rockefeller laughed. "Lord, Chauncey, that's pocket change. Keep it for yourself. God knows, you deserve it."

Helen Lee asked a woman's question. "What do you think will happen to Thornton?"

"Do you care?" Drake asked.

"No, not really."

"He'll die or somebody will kill him."

Rockefeller nodded. "Serves him right, I say."

Chapter 63

Drake and the others rode into Green Meadow three days later.

Apart from some boarded-up windows and bullet holes in the timbers of the storefronts, the town had largely survived the Fat Man's attack unscathed.

At the Bon-Ton Hotel, Otto Grunwald, a bandage around his head, accepted Drake with open arms after Rockefeller assured the manager that Mr. Drake was now a gentleman of considerable means.

Drake nodded to the bandage after he'd signed the register. "Did you get that during the fight, Otto?"

"Yes, Mr. Drake. I stuck my head out the door to take a look at what was happening and some rooster tried to blow it off."

"Happens in gunfights," Rockefeller said.

"Poor Marshal Halloran wasn't so lucky."

"Wounded?"

"Dead as a doorknob. They say the desperado Harvey Thornton shot him."

"Anyone else I know?"

"Peter J. Grapples was wounded. Ed Winslow is dead with three others. Sy Goldberg is laid up, shot seven times, they say. I heard he was always in the midst of the fray, so no wonder."

"Ah, *mein* goot friends. You're safe, safe at last."

Karl Benz came running down the stairs, and Rockefeller regarded him with genuine pleasure.

"How are you, Karl?" he said, extending his hand.

"I am well, John. The shoulder hurts, but not too bad."

Benz shook hands with Drake, then hugged Helen Lee.

"Karl, did you meet the cavalry?" the woman asked.

"No *soldaten*, not a trace. I don't think they left Fort Sill, or they were sent elsewhere on more pressing military business."

"The president will hear of this," Rockefeller said, looking hot. "Heads will roll."

Benz turned to Drake. "Well, *mein kamerad*?"

"Well, what?"

"What happened? Is Harvey Thornton dead, and what of your *fraulein*?

"It's a long story, Karl."

"And you're tired, I know."

"Nancy is dead, the Fat Man's dead, and Thornton wishes he was. That's the short version."

Benz, shaken to the core, struggled for words, but Rockefeller relieved him of that burden.

"Karl, will you accompany Miss Lee and myself back to Washington? We still have much business to discuss."

The German found his voice. "Yes, John, of course I will."

Then, with ponderous Teutonic sympathy, he hugged

Drake close, then held him at arm's length, reading his eyes.

"I am so sorry, Chauncey. Words cannot express . . ."

Drake smiled. "I know, Karl." At a loss for words himself, he added, "I know."

He turned to Grunwald and held out his hand. "My key, Otto."

"Before you go, Chauncey, I have something to say," Rockefeller said. "When I get back to Washington I plan to ask the president to strike you a gold medal for services to our great nation."

Helen Lee smiled. "Why, that's a wonderful idea." She laid her hand on Drake's shoulder. "No one deserves a medal more than you do, Chauncey."

There were ways to answer that. Drake could have said what he was thinking, that every medal casts a shadow, no matter how much it glitters.

But he did not.

"Thank you," he said. "I surely appreciate it."

"I plan to leave tomorrow, Chauncey," Rockefeller said. "Will you join us for dinner tonight?"

"Yes," Drake said, "I'd be honored." He bowed to Helen Lee. "Now, if you will excuse me."

He climbed the stairs, saddlebags over his shoulder, and walked into his room. He felt old, and impossibly tired.

It had been in Drake's mind to sleep a few hours, but one glance in the room's full-length mirror convinced him otherwise.

The band of the dead man's hat came down to just above his eyebrows and his clothes hung on him, dirty, dusty, and shabby. The bloodstained bandage on his hand was filthy, his cheeks sunken and bearded, his eyes hollow.

He smiled at his image.

"Chauncey," he said, "you're a sight to see."

He had things to do, one of them to find Nancy's body if he could, but visiting the bank, then Dr. Rosewell, and buying new clothes were immediate priorities.

Drake picked up his saddlebags from the bed and stepped out of his room and into the street.

Since the banker Peter J. Grapples was indisposed, the transaction was handled by an assistant, who gave Drake a receipt for a deposit of twenty-one thousand dollars.

"Please stop by for a sherry and cigars sometime, Mr. Drake," the assistant beamed. "We'll always be happy to see you."

Drake nodded and waved a hand. *How times change,* he thought.

"You've healed well," Dr. Rosewell said. "I've replaced the bandage to keep the wounds clean, but come back and see me in a few days."

He looked puzzled. "We're having an epidemic of amputated fingers recently. It's quite remarkable in fact."

Suddenly Drake was alert. "Who else?"

"A Pinkerton detective named Reuben Withers who has become better known, around here at least, as the hero of the battle of Green Meadow."

Drake rose to his feet, his face shocked. "Reuben is still alive?"

"He was alive when he left my surgery yesterday. But in these parlous times, who knows?"

"Where is he?"

"At this time of the afternoon, he usually plays chess with Peter J. Grapples. Mr. Grapples took a bullet in the battle and remains quite poorly."

"I have to go, Doctor," Drake said, heading for the door. "I'll see you in a few days."

"Perhaps we can discuss a prosthesis then."

Drake opened the door and looked back. "Oh, sure," he said. "That's what we'll discuss about."

Chapter 64

Grapples's wife, a thin woman who looked at Drake as though someone was holding a dead fish under her nose, led him to her husband's bedroom.

She opened the door and said, "Mr. Grapples, there's a person here to see you."

"Well, show him inside, Matilda," Grapples said.

"Don't stay long," the woman warned.

A devil in him, Drake pulled the bank statement from his shirt pocket, unfolded the paper, and held it up to the woman's face.

"Stay as long as you like," Matilda said. "Will it be coffee or tea?"

When Drake stepped inside, Withers rose to meet him, a wide grin on his face.

"Chauncey, I never thought I'd see you again," he said, hugging Drake close.

"And I thought you were dead."

"I came near." He waved a hand. "Do you know Mr. Grapples?"

"Mr. Drake and I are old acquaintances," the banker said.

Drake had questions to ask, but politeness demanded he inquire about the health of the sick. "How are you feeling, Peter?" he asked.

"I took a bullet in the brisket, but thanks to Dr. Rosewell, I'm on the mend." Grapples looked at Drake's hand. "Yet more of Harvey Thornton's work?"

"Yeah, he shot up Reuben and me at the same time."

"Detective Withers saved the town, you know," Grapples said. "Even though he was more dead than alive by the time he got here."

The banker moved the chessboard off his legs. "By the way, Chauncey, you look like you should be riding the bed wagon your own self."

"I've been through it," Drake said.

"Take a seat. Tell us," Grapples said.

Drake gratefully sank into an overstuffed chair.

"I want to hear Reuben's story first."

"There's not much to tell," Withers said.

"Start with why you left me."

"I knew I'd be a burden to you, Chauncey, so I waited until you were asleep and wandered off into the woods."

Withers sat on the corner of the bed. "Finally, I lay down under a tree and waited to die."

"Brave man, Detective," Grapples said. "Brave fellow, indeed."

"Well," Withers said, "I woke up and to my surprise I wasn't dead. I got to my feet and started walking. I don't know how I got here, but I finally reached Green Meadow."

"Dub Halloran wanted to throw Mr. Withers in jail,"

Grapples said. "But I spoke up for him. I said any man who wanders into a town missing the fingers of his left hand and almost dead, is inclined to tell the truth."

Withers grinned. "It wasn't that easy convincing folks, even then. But Sy Goldberg and a few of the other merchants took me seriously enough to organize a defense."

"As a precaution, you understand," Grapples said.

"Yes, after warning me that if I was telling a big windy, they'd hang me," Withers said.

"Merely another precaution," Grapples said, waving a hand, looking not in the least nonplussed.

"So the Fat Man attacked," Drake said. "What then?"

"Sy Goldberg organized the defense," Withers said. "He was a brigadier general in the late war, you know. Anyway, when mercenaries go up against desperate men who are fighting for their homes and families, they seldom prevail."

"How many did they lose?" Drake said.

Withers and Grapples exchanged glances and the banker coughed. He waited, then realized Withers was not going to speak.

"Twenty-one in the actual battle, another twenty-three during the . . . ah, rout."

"Wounded?"

"There were no wounded."

"Good shooting," Drake said, his words dry as dust.

"Remember, we lost five men, Chauncey," Withers said. "Some of those Texas boys were game, and surrender was not an option."

Cups rattled in saucers; then Mrs. Grapples entered with a tray.

"I'll serve," she said.

"My, my, Matilda, our best china?"

The woman laid the tray on a table and stepped to the bed. She whispered into her husband's ear, and Grapples immediately sat higher on his pillows.

"Some cake for Mr. Drake, my dear—the nice yellow one with the chocolate icing you baked yesterday."

"I'll bring it right away," the woman said.

"Now . . . Chauncey . . . no point in being formal here," Grapples said, after he'd seen Drake supplied with tea and cake, "tell us of your adventures. I have no doubt that, in the course of them, you played a most gallant role."

Drake told of the death of the Fat Man and his maiming of Harvey Thornton. He did not mention Nancy, an open wound that would never heal, nor how he had acquired his money.

"Then the ringleader is dead, a fate he richly deserved," Grapples said.

Drake nodded. "The Fat Man took one step too far when he declared war on a bunch of farmers and storekeepers."

Grapples grinned. "And Brigadier General Sy Goldberg."

"And a down-on-his-luck gambler by the name of Chauncey Drake," Withers said. He raised his teacup. "Here's to you, Chauncey."

Chapter 65

"Look at me, Chauncey, all shot to pieces," Sy Goldberg said.

He was sitting behind his counter in a chair that spilled horsehair and smelled like mummy dust.

"You remember the hogs, Chauncey? They all went bad on me and the coyotes ate them. Sold my beer at a loss, and it well-nigh ruined me. Then four of my best customers were killed in the battle, and you out somewhere with nothing to pawn. Oy, how can I stay in business?"

"You look just fine, Sy," Drake said. He glanced around at well-stocked shelves. "So does the store."

"Fine, he says, and me shot to doll rags and my miserable goods covered in spiderwebs. Have you seen my wife, Chauncey? Rags. Dressed in rags. And she's starving. She's lost two of her chins and the third is threatening to go."

"I'm sorry to see you and Mrs. Goldberg so low, Sy," Drake said.

"Low, he says. I'm lower than low. Hard times have

come down, Chauncey." His shrewd black eyes lifted to Drake's face. "Unless maybe you're here to do business?"

"I'm here to buy," Drake said. "Suits, shirts, shoes, underwear, a hat. I need everything."

Goldberg jumped to his feet, displaying surprising nimbleness for a man who was at death's door just a moment before.

"Ah, Chauncey, you know I don't care about money, but do you have any?"

Drake took a roll from his pocket and waved it in Goldberg's face.

"Chauncey, you're in luck," the storekeeper beamed. "I just got a shipment of gentlemen's clothing from Brooks Brothers of New York that I'm selling wholesale to the public."

He spread his hands and shrugged. "Seconds, you understand, but you can look at these garments until your eyes ache and you won't find a split seam or a badly tailored lapel. And shirts of the best Egyptian linen, shoes from London, England, underwear of the finest wool, and hats all the way from Boston town."

"Well, let's get started, Sy," Drake said. He spread his arms. "Get your tape. I'm all yours."

"Mind, everything's at cost to my friends, Chauncey. That's why I'll end up in the poor house."

Six months later a package addressed to Chauncey Drake, Esq., was delivered to the Bon-Ton Hotel.

Since Drake was riding a winning streak and had left for pastures new, Sy Goldberg, the lion of Green Meadow, took it in charge.

The package included a brief note from the president thanking him for services rendered, and the medal itself, pure gold—Sy determined—said only: FOR MERITORIOUS SERVICE.

The front of the medal bore a portrait of President Harrison, the reverse a mighty battleship with all guns blazing.

"Why a boat?" Otto Grunwald asked.

Goldberg smiled. "A Navy reject, I imagine, struck for some dead admiral or other."

"Do you have a forwarding address for Mr. Drake?"

Goldberg shook his head. "No, I don't. But he's a gambler and once he loses all his money he'll be back to see me."

He smiled at Grunwald. "Men like Chauncey Drake, they always come back."

Read on for an excerpt
from Ralph Compton's classic

WHISKEY RIVER

Coming in January 2011 from Signet.

Waco, Texas. June 25, 1866.

After four long years they were coming home.

Mark Rogers and Bill Harder had much in common. While still young men, they had "learned cow" together in south Texas. When they were of age, they each had "proved up" on a half section of land, just north of Waco, on opposite banks of the Brazos River. The combined half sections were an ideal spread, with the Brazos providing abundant water. But when the war came and Texas seceded, Mark and Bill answered the call of the Confederacy, each just a few days shy of twenty-five. Now, after four long years of war, they neared Waco. They were self-conscious, for they were dressed in rags, which had once been the proud uniforms of the Confederacy. Neither man was armed, and for lack of saddles they rode mules bareback. Mark Rogers and Bill Harder were as gaunt as the animals they rode. When they rode in, Waco didn't *look* any different, but somehow, it felt all wrong. They reined up before Bradley's Mercantile. Ab Bradley had known them all their lives, and as they entered the store, he came limping to meet them.

"My soul and body," Ab said. "Mark Rogers and Bill Harder. I heard you was dead."

"There was times when we wished we were, Ab," said Mark. "Better that than rotting away in a Yankee prison."

"Yeah," Bill agreed. "All we have is these rags we're wearin', and two poor old mules as hungry as we are. The Yankees stomped hell out of us, took our guns, and sent us back with our tails between our legs. We heard soldiers would be comin' to put us under martial law until the Congress can decide what our punishment should be. Has any of 'em showed up?"

"They have," said Ab gravely. "There's already a full company of them in Austin. But that's not the problem. The problem is the newly appointed tax collectors. First thing they done was reassess everybody's spreads, and them that couldn't pay lost everything. They started out takin' what belonged to those of you who went to war."

"The sons of bitches," Mark said. "We wasn't here. They've taken our spread?"

"Yours, and a dozen others, all up and down the Brazos," said Ab. "They're bein' held by men armed with scatterguns."

"By God," Bill said, "we'll organize the rest of the rightful owners and raise hell."

"I don't think so," said Ab. "Riley Wilkerson, Mike Duvall, and Ellis Van Horn tried to do exactly that. Without weapons, they attacked armed men and were shot down like stray dogs. The others that come back saw how it was, and left, traveling west. You can fight, but you can't win."

"Legalized murder, then," Mark said.

"That's what I'd call it," said Ab, "but I wouldn't say it too loud."

"Ab," said Bill, "we don't have a peso between us, and I don't know when we'll be able to pay you, but we need grub. Can you help us?"

"Some," Ab said cautiously. "The state's been up against a blockade, and supply lines still ain't open. All I got is homegrown beef, beans, and bacon. No coffee, salt, or sugar."

"We'll accept whatever you can spare, and be thankful," said Mark.

"You don't aim to back off, then, do you?" Ab asked.

"Hell no," said Mark. "I don't know what we'll do, but by the Eternal, we'll be doing something."

"Just be careful, boys," Ab said.

"We're obliged to you for the warning," said Bill. "At least we won't be walking into it cold."

Ab filled two gunnysacks with supplies. Mark and Bill thanked the old man and left the store. Nobody paid any attention to the two riders as they rode south. Darkness was several hours away, and they road into a stand of cottonwood where there was a spring they remembered.

"Whatever bronc we have to ride," Mark said, "I'll feel better jumpin' on it with a full belly."

There was lush graze near the river, and the half-starved mules took advantage of it. Mark and Bill built a small fire over which they broiled bacon. Their meager meal finished, the angry duo set about making plans to reclaim their holdings.

"From what Ab told us," said Bill, "there shouldn't be more than two of these varmints with scatterguns guardin' our spread, and we'll likely find one of 'em holed up in my shack and the other in yours. We can take 'em one at a time and get our hands on them scatterguns."

"That'll bring the soldiers," Mark said. "We can't stand off the damn army with a pair of scatterguns. Besides, we were granted amnesty by signing pledges not to take up arms against the Union."

"Soldiers and amnesty be damned," said Bill. "Just because they beat us don't give 'em the right to move in and rob us blind while we're not here to defend what's ours. Soon as it's dark enough, I'm movin' in. You comin' with me?"

"I reckon," Mark said. "We'll likely light more fires than we can put out, but we can't just let them pick us clean. Hell, we'll do what we have to."

When darkness had fallen, they could see a distant light in the window of each of their shacks. They first approached Bill's spread, and in the dim light from a window, they saw the dark shadow of a horse tied outside the shack.

"You spook the horse," said Bill, "and I'll get him as he comes out the door."

Taking a handful of rocks, Mark began pelting the horse. It nickered, reared, and then nickered again. It had the desired effect. The door swung open, and the man with the scattergun started out. In an instant Bill had an arm around his throat and a death grip on the muzzle of the shotgun. He drove a knee into the man's groin, who, with a gasp of pain, released the shotgun. As he doubled up in agony, Bill seized the shotgun's stock and slammed it under the unfortunate man's chin.

"One of 'em down," said Bill with satisfaction.

"God almighty," Mark said, kneeling by the fallen man, "his neck's broke. He's dead."

"I didn't shoot him," said Bill, more shaken than he wanted to admit. "I promised that I wouldn't take up arms, and I didn't."

"We can't leave him here," Mark said. "What do you aim to do with him?"

"Leave him where he is for now," said Bill. "He ain't goin' nowhere. After we've took care of the varmint at your place, we'll dispose of the both of them where they'll never be found. Nobody can prove anything against us."

"Maybe you're right," Mark said. "We've gone too far to back out now."

Mark and Bill found a shallows and crossed the Brazos on foot, Mark carrying the confiscated shotgun.

"Give me the scattergun," said Bill. "If this one goes sour, I'll do the shootin'. So far, they got nothin' on you."

"No," Mark said. "This is my place. I won't have you takin' a rap for what I should have done. This time, you spook the horse, and I'll get the drop when the varmint comes bustin' out."

Bill began antagonizing the picketed horse, and the animal reacted predictably. But the animal's owner didn't come busting through the front door. He came around the corner of the house, and Bill threw himself facedown just in time to avoid a lethal blast from the scattergun. Like an echo, Mark fired, and the deadly charge caught the guard in the chest. He collapsed like a crumpled sack.

"My God," Bill said, "now we're into it."

"So we are," said Mark. "Would you feel better if I'd let him cut you in two with that cannon?"

"This is no time for damned foolishness," Bill said. "There's still a chance we can get out of this if we can stash this pair where they'll never be found, and we got to do it fast. There'll be rain before morning, and it'll cover our trail. Get a blanket from inside. We don't want blood all over this hombre's saddle when his horse shows up somewhere."

Riding their mules, they each led a horse with a dead man slung over the saddle. Far down the Brazos, they disposed of both dead men in a bog hole that overflowed from the river.

"A damned shame, lettin' these horses and saddles go, while we're ridin' a broke-down pair of old mules," said Mark.

"Hell of a lot easier than explaining to the law where we got the horses and saddles," Bill replied.

Just for a moment, the moon peeked from behind the gathering clouds, and turning, Mark looked back.

"What are you lookin' at?" Bill asked.

"Them horses," said Mark. "They're following us."

"Won't matter," Bill replied. "There'll be rain before daylight."

But the shotgun blasts had been heard at the old Duvall place, and by the time Mark and Bill returned to Bill's shack, they had unwanted company. While the pair still had the weapons they had taken from the dead men, they had no chance to use them. A cold voice from the darkness spoke.

"You're covered, and there's three of us. Drop the guns and step down."

Mark Rogers and Bill Harder had no choice. Dropping the shotguns, they slid off their mules.

"You got nothing on us," Bill said angrily. "These are our spreads, proved up before we went to war."

"And confiscated for nonpayment of taxes," said the hostile voice.

"What do you aim to do with us?" Mark asked.

"Turn you over to the military, come morning," said their antagonist. "We heard the shooting. Now you coyotes show up with a pair of shotguns and the horses followin' you that belonged to Pritchett and Wade. We don't know what you done with 'em, but there's enough evidence for the law to consider 'em dead."

"Yeah," said a second voice with an ugly laugh, "they'll be the first ex-Rebs to face up to a military firing squad."

The unfortunate duo was marched into Bill's cabin, where they were bound hand and foot. They were shoved roughly against a wall, where they slid down to uncomfortable sitting positions.

"My name's Crowder," said the most talkative of their trio of antagonists. "Gortner and Preemo will keep you company and see that you don't get any ideas. I'll telegraph the military at Austin, and there'll be soldiers here by tomorrow."

"A writer in the tradition of Louis L'Amour
and Zane Grey!"
—*Huntsville Times*

National Bestselling Author

RALPH COMPTON

AUTUMN OF THE GUN
THE KILLING SEASON
THE DAWN OF FURY
BULLET CREEK
RIO LARGO
DEADWOOD GULCH
A WOLF IN THE FOLD
TRAIL TO COTTONWOOD FALLS
BLUFF CITY
THE BLOODY TRAIL
SHADOW OF THE GUN
DEATH OF A BAD MAN
RIDE THE HARD TRAIL
BLOOD ON THE GALLOWS
BULLET FOR A BAD MAN
THE CONVICT TRAIL
RAWHIDE FLAT
OUTLAW'S RECKONING
THE BORDER EMPIRE
THE MAN FROM NOWHERE
SIXGUNS AND DOUBLE EAGLES
BOUNTY HUNTER
FATAL JUSTICE
STRYKER'S REVENGE
DEATH OF A HANGMAN
NORTH TO THE SALT FORK
DEATH RIDES A CHESTNUT MARE
RUSTED TIN

**Available wherever books are sold or at
penguin.com**

S543

No other series packs this much heat!

THE TRAILSMAN

#320: OREGON OUTRAGE
#321: FLATHEAD FURY
#322: APACHE AMBUSH
#323: WYOMING DEATHTRAP
#324: CALIFORNIA CRACKDOWN
#325: SEMINOLE SHOWDOWN
#326: SILVER MOUNTAIN SLAUGHTER
#327: IDAHO GOLD FEVER
#328: TEXAS TRIGGERS
#329: BAYOU TRACKDOWN
#330: TUCSON TYRANT
#331: NORTHWOODS NIGHTMARE
#332: BEARTOOTH INCIDENT
#333: BLACK HILLS BADMAN
#334: COLORADO CLASH
#335: RIVERBOAT RAMPAGE
#336: UTAH OUTLAWS
#337: SILVER SHOWDOWN
#338: TEXAS TRACKDOWN
#339: RED RIVER RECKONING
#340: HANNIBAL RISING
#341: SIERRA SIX-GUNS
#342: ROCKY MOUNTAIN REVENGE
#343: TEXAS HELLIONS
#344: SIX-GUN GALLOWS
#345: SOUTH PASS SNAKE PIT
#346: ARKANSAS AMBUSH
#347: DAKOTA DEATH TRAP
#348: BACKWOODS BRAWL
#349: NEW MEXICO GUN-DOWN

Follow the trail of Penguin's Action Westerns at
penguin.com/actionwesterns